S0-DNG-687

Woodley Park

Douglas J. Simms

American Literary Press
Five Star Special Edition
Baltimore, Maryland

Woodley Park

Copyright © 2006 Douglas J. Simms

All rights reserved under International and Pan-American copyright conventions. No part of this book may be reproduced, stored in a retrieval system, or transmitted in any form, electronic, mechanical, or other means, now known or hereafter invented, without written permission of the publisher. Address all inquiries to the publisher. All opinions expressed herein are those of the author and do not, necessarily, represent those of the publisher.

Library of Congress
Cataloging-in-Publication Data
ISBN 1-56167-922-4

Library of Congress Card Catalog Number:
2005909136

Published by

American Literary Press
Five Star Special Edition
8019 Belair Road, Suite 10
Baltimore, Maryland 21236

Manufactured in the United States of America

Many guitarists refer to their guitar as their lover.

Some call it their ax.

Prologue

A man with peppered-gray hair and a matching, tweed blazer walks down a busy D.C. sidewalk clutching his satchel of paintings in his right arm. He flails his left at nothing and says, "Leave me alone." He bends his head down and meanders back and forth across the sidewalk, bumping into to people. He almost falls. He holds his satchel of art with both his arms and then stops in front of a few graduate students sitting on a bench.

"Just leave me alone," he yells.

The students stop laughing and look up at him. He has dark circles beneath his lifeless eyes that blankly gaze at the oncoming traffic. His hands knead the satchel.

"I've had it with you. You damn bitch." He continues walking.

The students look to see who he was talking to and see nothing.

"What is with that dude," says one of the students.

"Yeah, what's going on in his head?"

The man takes the escalator down to the Metro tracks beneath the city. He stands waiting and clutching his paintings. The white lights next to the track begin flashing. The satchel slips from his hand and onto the tracks. He smiles and jumps in front of the oncoming train.

Woodley Park

The fact that I was on the list to testify as an eye witness at the hearing twenty-four years ago regarding the deaths of my father and brother disturbed me since I had not been present when Francis the Ax Man killed them. I was fifteen then.

Now, I tried to focus on driving away from the sullen clouds of southern Virginia, away from Picketsville, away from where I grew up. I wasn't sure if both my hands were on the steering wheel to combat the gusts of wind along those back roads, or to steady my resolve and hurried pace to get back to D.C. for my graduate school class that night. The temperature gage in my old, silver BMW dinged and flashed to indicate that the temperature had fallen below thirty-eight degrees, when ice can form on the roads, hidden in the speckles on the asphalt.

I soon arrived at our townhouse in the Maryland suburbs of D.C. I hurried through a shower, skipped a shave and put on the warmest clothes I owned--long underwear, blue jeans, two heavy shirts, a thick brown sweater and hiking boots. Downstairs, I stuffed my assignments into my briefcase and checked the locks on the doors. I backed out of the garage and turned on the radio. I drove toward the main road, but at the main entrance to the development, I turned around and drove back by our townhouse. The garage was closed.

It was rush hour, and the weekly evening accident on the interstate north, toward the mountains, had completely stopped the commuters. Fortunately, I was heading south, into D.C. I parked at the nearest Metro station, and the radio antenna hummed down. I had forgotten to turn up the sound. I bought a fare card, bound up the escalator and boarded the subway train. Sitting on the hideous, pumpkin-colored seat, I opened my briefcase and pulled out the research documents, what little I had acquired from the Picketsville courthouse. The research for my thesis involved the school closings in sixty-four as a result of a federal mandate to integrate public schools, but the documents were sparse or allegedly in storage. So too were the documents regarding the execution of Francis the Ax Man. The subway train offered a few unsettling tremors as we entered the tunnels.

I glanced around at the various characters on the train--all different types of people. I was never sure whether or not to make eye contact with other passengers. Across the aisle sat a businessman reading the paper. His blond hair was combed perfectly, and his light-gray suit appeared to exist on a manikin--smooth, perfect. In front of me twitched a leather-clad kid with blue, spiked hair. Underneath fuzzy, blond eyebrows, his unblinking slate-blue eyes stared back at me. The businessman adjusted his tie and ruffled the paper to the next page. Nearby slept a ragged, rubbery person swaying back and forth in rhythm to the train's wobbles. Then his cigarette fell from its perch on the top of his ear and rolled away from us both.

The whirring sound of the train against the tracks increased as we sped through the dimly lit tunnels underneath D.C. After staring blankly at the documents for several stops, I returned them to my briefcase. I looked up, and the blue-haired passenger's hair now seemed yellow.

We had just passed the Woodley Park Station, and the next stop was my stop, Dupont Circle. We wound through the dark tunnel. Suddenly the train stopped between stations, deep under the city. The passengers nervously glanced at each other and me, and I at them. We sat for a few disturbing minutes.

The driver announced a "signal problem."

"What the hell is a signal problem?" The scratchy voice came from directly behind me. We sat and waited. "We have a signal problem," said the conductor. "There's been an accident at Dupont Circle." The passengers began to groan and murmur. The businessman rustled his paper. The lights flickered.
        The driver's voice crackled through the speaker. "We have to turn around. I'll be walking the train."
        A few minutes later, the red metal door slammed behind me, and he walked by. The groans and sighs increased. The rubbery soul shifted in his sickly tomato-colored seat and half opened his bloodshot eyes. "Fuckin' Metro," he muttered.
        The train reversed course back toward Woodley Park. A sudden jolt slid a pale-green umbrella under my legs. I picked it up and turned around. Directly behind me sat an elderly woman with a deathly stare in her colorless eyes.
        "Is this yours?" I handed her the umbrella.
        She took the umbrella. "Hmmpf, signal problems." She turned her wrinkled face toward the darkened window.
        The driver told us to exit the train at Woodley Park. The damp odor of this unknown stop filled my nostrils. I followed the other passengers to the stairs. People walked in front of me, bumped me and seemed generally irritated--as was I. We herded onto the final escalator, and I heard someone making a moo sound from below. The freezing rain striking the top of the escalator and my uncovered head quelled my grin.
        Seemingly confused and disgruntled people crammed the exit, but I found some refuge from the ice blizzard under an overhang of a building and walked over to a tall fellow in a camel-colored overcoat. He lit a cigarette.
        "Which direction is Dupont Circle?" I asked.

He blew out some smoke and shrugged his large shoulders. "I've never been here before."

The cabs were jammed. The busses were full. I wasn't sure which side of Connecticut Avenue the subway opening had left me. I struggled with my umbrella and guessed. As I walked, the wind smarted my face with pellets of frozen water, and I struggled to keep the umbrella from its violent grasp. The strap of my brief case kept sliding off my shoulder as it too became soaked and frigid. I happened upon a woman, perhaps a girl, and asked directions. She wore no coat, only a turquoise sweater and black slacks. The sight of her drenched sweater sent a shiver through me.

"Excuse me. Is this the way downtown?" I asked as politely as I could.

Her eyes glazed. She stepped back, then offered a half smile. "Yes," she said.

"Across the bridge?" A gust of wind splattered us both with more icy rain.

She stepped to her left, wrapped one arm across her breasts, and looked toward the bridge with a twitch, "Yes."

I smiled. "Thank you." I paused and gazed at her icy, hay-colored hair. I moved my black umbrella toward her.

"We can share," I said.

She stepped back, and folded her other arm across her breasts. "No...no thanks."

I left her standing on the pale cement sidewalk, crossed the intersection and was soon on the bridge where the wind and sleet, unfettered by buildings or trees, assaulted me. I quickened my pace and fought to keep the umbrella from the clutches of the wind. The cold, damp air filled my nostrils and pained my sinuses. Far below, horns blasted from cars carrying people who probably just wanted to be home and warm. I just wanted to get to class on time.

The bridge had never seemed that long in a car. The ice and rain seared my face. I could no longer distinguish between the pain of heat or cold as I neared the large stone lion at the end of the bridge. The buildings ahead seemed to offer some refuge from the wind. I turned and saw the girl walking behind me. I continued toward the lion and decided that I couldn't blame the girl for being cautious. The road forked after the bridge. I stood examining the road signs and checking the passing cabs.

"Help!" I heard.

I turned around. A gust of sleet sliced into my face, and I almost lost the umbrella to the wind. The girl was no longer behind me. The wind whistled past my reddened ears. My briefcase, heavier from the rain, slid off my shoulder again. I squinted into the darkness behind me--nothing. Headlights dimmed my view and shrank my pupils. I turned back around and looked down both forks--only darkness. A passing cab let out a loud honk at a slow driver. Water and ice splashed onto my jeans. I took a step. The street lamp dimly lit the way toward my left.

"Help."

It sounded like it came from my previous path. I folded the umbrella and ran back toward the lion. I could see only the headlights of the cars shimmering off the watery, black pavement. I reached the lion and stopped to listen. It stared into my eyes, cold, powerful. It seemed taller before, stared down at me. I heard a muffled voice just below the bridge. I drew my umbrella, my only weapon, and fought the gusts of sleet into the darkness which was intermittently illuminated by flashes of light from the cars below. I stood about halfway down the hill on the slippery, dormant grass and adjusted my eyes to the darkness. The wind swayed the frozen tree limbs and almost forced me off my feet, but my footing seemed adapted to the slope. To my right stood the supports for the lion's bridge, and to the left, a patch of iced, lifeless bushes and trees. I listened.

I crept into the den of bushes and heard rustling. Headlights splintered through the glittering tree limbs revealing her half-naked body on the icy grass. I knelt beside her, but she kicked me away. I slid down the slippery hill until I grabbed the base of a bush. I regained my breath and crawled back up. Another honking car passed below. Her eyes were partially open staring blankly up into the dripping tree limbs. Her sweater was ripped almost completely off. Blood oozed from her nose. I tried to replace her clothing, cover her, warm her.

"It's all right," I said.

I took off my coat and wrapped it around her. A noise startled me. She started pounding on my chest with her fists.

"Get away. Get away."

I wrapped my arms around her.

"It's all right. He's gone. He's gone. Shhhh." After she pushed a few more times, she became limp in my arms.

"It'll be all right." My voice wavered.

We were both covered in sleet. I carried her up the hill. Exhausted, I stopped and tried to warm her. She woke.

"What are you doing?" She pushed me.

"Easy. You're okay. I just need to rest. Here's your purse." She struggled to get away. I let her go. She stumbled a few steps and tripped just below the lion.

I reached her and turned her over. She started to flail her arms against me.

"Stop," she said.

"Wait. It wasn't me. Look at me." I shook her.
"Look."

Her eyes frantically darted back and forth.

"I'm the guy with the umbrella...remember?" Her
arms fell from my chest to her sides. "We need to get you
warm."

"I live just down the block. I'll be fine."

"You can hardly walk." I knelt beside her, and the
lion looked more familiar from my knees.

We rose beneath it and, with her leaning against
me, walked down the slippery sidewalk. Cabs sped down
the avenue, and the sleet pelted us as we staggered along.
The stone-faced buildings slowly passed as the ice and
wind relentlessly assaulted our progress. We arrived at
her building, both of us soaked. She pressed the buzzer.

"Who is it?" asked the guard through the little
speaker.

"It's Susan."

The lock on the glass door clicked, and she
handed me my coat.

"But..."

She looked at me with glazed, murky eyes.

"I don't even know your name," I said, and I
forced my way through the closing door.

She pulled her torn clothes around her and
looked back. "Leave me alone." She quickened her steps.

"I want to make sure..." The elevator opened. She
hurried in and started to frantically push the third floor
button, but I hopped into the elevator. The doors closed.

"Why won't you leave me alone?" Her eyes rolled,
and she dropped like a stone to the floor of the elevator.
Her purse fell at my feet, and its contents spilled out. I
grabbed her apartment keys, # 302, and stuffed the rest of
the items back into her purse. When the doors opened on
the third floor, I picked her up and looked for her
apartment. I opened the door with her key, turned on a

7

light and laid her gently on the sofa. I looked around her apartment and found a towel, a pillow and a comforter. I dried her hair, wrapped her in the comforter and placed the towel covered pillow under her head. I noted her phone number and her name, Susan Toller.

She awoke and started screaming. I embraced her, trying to warm her frozen, trembling body. She pushed me back. I grabbed her shoulders, and eventually she calmed. With Susan quiet, wrapped in her comforter, I set the door to lock behind me and ventured back out into February's gloom.

I was late for class of course. I entered the room after the fifteen-block walk through the storm. I tried to be quiet and unobtrusive, but the eyes of my classmates showed their questions and their dismay at my condition. They saw the water and ice sliding off my dirty-blond hair and some noticed the brown and green stains on my clothes. I sat and tried to listen to the discussion, evidently regarding Kafka's *Metamorphosis*. However, my thoughts remained at Woodley Park.

Break came not too soon despite my tardy arrival. After buying a cup of coffee, I returned to the classroom where everyone was talking about the Metro accident. I listened and rubbed my hands together for warmth until class resumed.

"What is the definition of irony?" The professor asked.

"Lions protecting something that they cannot protect," I said.

The professor looked at me across the rims of his glasses. "What?"

"I'm sorry. Never mind."

At the end of the class, the professor reminded us of our next assignment and asked us to consider whether or not the narrator in Dostoyevsky's *Notes From the Underground* likes himself. I turned in a soggy paper. We had identified problems but solved none, with one exception. The train had probably stopped due to someone's using the stop at Dupont Circle for his own pleasure or amusement. The Dupont stop was still closed, so I took a cab to Woodley Park. Seven bucks later, Woodley Park was also closed.

"The next stop may be open," the driver said with a thick Jamaican accent.

"Okay. Let's try. Do you know what happened?" The cab's wipers methodically swished ice and rain off the windshield.

"Some guy jumped in front of the train, man. Pretty rude to do it at rush hour. No consideration."

I wished that I had gone to the bank earlier as I had planned. At that rate, a ride home would cost at least fifty more than I had. We went to the next stop, and it was open. I paid the driver with a generous tip that perhaps expressed my relief more than my thanks.

I sat in the horribly orange seat and could only wonder about Susan. The train reached the end of the line where my car was parked. The driver's door was frozen shut. I fought with it for a few minutes and then tried the passenger side, which eventually relinquished to my tugs, and I crawled in for the drive home. I couldn't see them, but I knew the road was littered with menacing patches of ice just on the surface, invisible but very much there, waiting.

Sandy had parked in the guest area so I could drive into the garage. The garage door rattled shut while I removed my boots before stepping into the basement. I heard the TV blaring upstairs in the living room which meant that my wife was still awake. I walked up the stairs and set my bag in the living room by my chair.

"How was school?" she said.

"Fine." I walked to the kitchen, popped a beer and walked back to my chair.

She sat to my right on a pale-white sofa a couple of feet from my adjacent leather chair. "What happened to you?" She looked at me as if I were some stranger. I began to shiver. Her warm, brown eyes widened under her reddish brown hair. "What's wrong, honey?" she asked.

"Is the local news on yet?" I set the beer on the table after a long gulp.

"In a few minutes."

"Did you hear about the Metro?"

She stood. "No." She walked to the kitchen for more ice and plinked it into her cup of soda. "Why?" she called from the neighboring kitchen.

"There was an incident."

She returned with her fizzing cup. "What?"

"I need to change." I walked up the stairs, removed my soaked clothes and took a long, hot shower. I fumbled with the soap and kept increasing the water temperature. The water and soap suds streamed down me, swirling into the drain at my feet.

"James? Are you all right?"

My head was against the steaming white tile. I grabbed the side of the shower stall, looked up and saw Sandy opening the shower door. She reached in and turned off the water. She gingerly handed me a towel.

"You have a scrape on your neck." I stepped out of the shower and dried. She went to the adjoining room, sat on the bed and watched me in the mirror. I returned the towel to its rod and walked past her. She was wearing the powder-blue, cotton pajamas that I had given her for Christmas.

"What happened? Did something happen in the storm?"

"Is the local news on yet?" I slipped on some jeans and a sweater.

"What's going on James? You were in the shower for…I was worried."

"Let's go downstairs and catch the news."

We sat separately. I noticed that the coffee table was covered with textbooks.

"I didn't know you read Jung," I said.

"I don't."

"But what are all these?" I pointed at the books strewn about the coffee table. "Why is Kafka out, Porosky, Dostoyevsky. You're not reading them are you?"

"Honey, I don't know why…I thought you were reading them."

I returned the books to their shelf and the local news came on, finally.

"James, did you eat? You look pale."

"Yes. Ham and cheese."

The broadcast began. Sandy sat up. "Can we change it to channel seven?"

I grabbed the remote. The channel seven anchor was smiling. "We have some weather headed our way. Also, there was a fatal accident at the Metro, and we a have a touching story about a missing pet. We'll tell you all about it after the break."

The only light in the room came from the flickering TV. Sandy sat directly opposite the TV and I against the adjacent wall. I walked into the kitchen and popped another beer. As I sat back down, the commercials stopped, and the newscaster with butter-colored hair began to speak. "Earlier this evening, a man threw himself in front of the Metro train at Dupont Circle." The newscast went to a live feed at Dupont Circle where a reporter interviewed several irritated travelers. After the reporter offered no information about what had happened on the Metro tracks below, she turned the newscast back over to the studio.

The anchor turned to his sidekick. "Well, Chip. This has been a real inconvenience for many commuters. A lot of people are upset."

"I don't blame them," said Chip. "Coming up, a cat finds a home. Don't go away. We'll be right back after these messages."

I looked over to Sandy. She leaned forward. "You were there?"

"Almost."

"Did you see it?"

"No. We had to backup to Woodley Park and get off. I ended up walking to class."

"In this weather?"

We sat through the pharmaceutical ads. I looked over at Sandy. "We'll know more about…about that stupid cat than the guy who, for some reason, decided to…" I stood, started toward the kitchen, but stopped next to her.

"James," she grabbed my arm, "let's just go to bed."

I caressed the back of her soft hair. "I'll be up in a minute."

She smiled at me and climbed the stairs. I flipped through the stations. Nothing more was reported about some mysterious soul who had decided that being mutilated by a train was the best thing to do that evening. After a few more beers, I went upstairs and quietly slid into bed where Sandy's snoring forced me to wrap the pillow around my ears, and I fell into a deep sleep.

I look out the second story bathroom window and see the clouds swirling, dark clouds. The Earth moves against the air, and the house rattles while strange creatures swoop through the air. Some are yellow. My father grabs me and throws me against the wall.

"Don't ever talk to your mother like that!"

The basement is full of boxes. I can't walk. My hands are missing again. I turn to my brother.
    "Are they still out there?"
    "Only the yellow ones," he says.
    "I need to get to my things."
    Father throws boxes into my path.
    "Damn you. That's unacceptable," I say.
    He looms over me. "Unacceptable, I'll show you unacceptable."
    I start to remove the boxes and throw them at him. He charges and grabs my throat. I push him away. I have my hands again. He lurches toward me.
    "Are they still out there?" I say.
    "Only the yellow ones," says Steve.
    Father is gone, and Steve crawls into a box. It closes.
    The clouds swirl, and still the Earth rumbles. I can't find my hands. The air is evaporating. I can't breath.
    "Susan, the air."
    The stone Lion opens his jaws. His yellow eyes gleam with beauty, with such beauty. He reaches his paw onto my shoulder. I kneel, looking for my hands. I need my hands. I look up into his jaws, his glowing eyes. He grins and licks his whiskers.
    "Is the air gone? Susan. If only you had shared. I could have. You wouldn't have to--"
    "James."
    "I'm so sorry I didn't--"
    "James. Wake up."
    The yellow monsters evaporate with the air.
    "James. Are you okay?"
    "Yes, Sandy. What time is it?"
    "Six. Who is Susan?"
    "I…I don't know."

That day, I went to a pay phone and called Susan-
-no answer. I tried several more times throughout the
week with no luck. The following Thursday, when I went
to class, I exited the train at Woodley Park. There was a
pay phone near the stop, and I phoned Susan but again,
no answer. I walked by her building, Susan's building,
and noticed that her name had been removed from the
buzzers.

Another week passed. I sat on the Metro, headed
for class. Snapshots, splinters of pain, crept into my
vision and into my thoughts. I could hear her screams, see
the fear in her eyes. The subway lights flashed by. A
young man in a sharp, charcoal-colored suit leaned
toward me.

"Would you look at this?" He pointed at the
newspaper.

"What?" I said.

"The night that idiot threw himself in front of the
train, a girl was raped and killed near the Woodley Park
stop."

"Yes?"

"She was only twenty, Susan Toller."

"Killed?" I looked at him.

"Strange though. It appears that the rapist carried
her back to her apartment, smothered her with a towel
covered pillow and then covered her in a blanket. But
this, this is the best part. He made a ham and cheese
sandwich, ate, dried her hair and locked the door behind
him when he left."

Sessions

I didn't know what to do regarding Susan's death. I considered calling the police. My finger prints and DNA samples were probably all over Susan's apartment. The police did not have my finger prints on file, and I decided to keep it that way. At first I felt confident that she was alive when I left, but the scene replayed in my mind as if its own thought process--like a computer program that constantly runs in the background. I tried to remember seeing her alive when I closed her apartment door, but my memories soon became blurred into the "what ifs" that a writer must constantly ask.

I remembered the words of a spiritual leader that I had hung out with many years before, a Swami. He had warned me that meditation is an investigation into both the dark and the light. He had not warned me about being a writer or an artist. I reached inside my own being to investigate how one person could rape and murder another. I attempted to write about it. I searched inside for how I could do such a thing, how I could possibly do it and not care, or worse yet, feel justified. Over the next two months, I slowly found the darkness inside me. I found the rage and fear. I became despondent and withdrawn from the outside world and remained in an interior world where violence not only made sense, but was also liberating. I developed a character whose only recourse to stop the emotional pain was to rape and murder an innocent girl. My obsession with this character frightened me. It seemed to disturb Sandy as well. She did not understand my need to write or understand that it was indeed work.

One spring weeknight, I waited up for Sandy. The late show ended, and she was still not home from work. I tried to console myself with the memory of her once leaving for the weekend without telling me. I waffled between anger and worry and tried to sleep on the couch by the phone. After a second sleepless night, I called her boss who was also wondering about her absence. I called her mother in New Jersey who knew nothing and now was worried as well. So, I called the police and reported Sandy missing. It made no sense. All of Sandy's things were still in our home, except Sandy and her purse. The police acted as if they were sympathetic, but their acting skills did little to calm my fears.

After a few more days of no word from the police and no sleep, I called Dr. Weiner. She scheduled a session for the next day. I needed to talk to someone, and my estranged family did not seem like an option. She had treated me nine years before for cocaine abuse.

The next day, I drove to Dr. Weiner's office in Rockville. A blond receptionist sat inside a Plexiglas room that appeared to be a checkpoint for the security wing of a hospital, and she seemed serious about her duties as the gatekeeper. She briefly removed the seemingly attached phone from the left side of her head, and I gave her my name. She waved me to have a seat. I sat on the tan leather chair and noticed my hands shaking and my stomach growling as I fumbled through the magazines on the table in front of me. Dr. Weiner poked her head around the corner.

"James." She stepped closer as I rose.

"Thank you for seeing me so quickly."

"Come on back. It is nice to see you." She waved her hand toward the hall, then led me to her office and closed the door. She looked the same. She had shoulder length, wavy, brown hair above her wide, brown eyes. Her large, round breasts pressed against a tight, white blouse. "Please have a seat."

I sat in the cream-colored chair and rubbed my
hands on my knees. "Looks like you've done well."
She smiled. "Yes." Her smile faded. "You
understand that after today, I must refer you to another
therapist due to what happened in my office the last time
we met." She crossed her silky legs and adjusted her
black skirt. "You sounded very upset on the phone
yesterday. I hope you have not had a relapse?"

"My wife…" Tears filled my eyes, and I looked
down at the powder-blue carpet.

"Take your time, James."

I was on the bottom of a swimming pool
searching for the side. The colors blurred and my
forehead pounded. Her blurry figure stood and put some
pink tissues in my hand. I gasped for air.

My vision returned, and I examined the room and
then her kind, searching eyes. She returned to her dark
leather chair.

"I can't sleep," I said.

"Are you having problems with your wife?"

"I lie down and can't quite get to sleep."

"Do you know why?" She uncrossed her legs and
leaned forward. My eyes automatically scanned her legs
and then glanced at the tops of her breasts that were
creeping out of her blouse. I looked at the pictures in the
room for a moment--Impressionists--collages of colors
blending and yet composed of independent dabs of paint.

"I twitch, my leg kicks, and I wake in a cold
sweat."

"Are you having nightmares?"

"Yes. I can see my..." I started rubbing my
forehead and eyes with my left hand, squeezing the moist
tissues in my right. "…I see Sandy. I see her bloody
body…"

"James?"

I was staring up at the bright-white ceiling.

"James, I'm right here." I turned my head and saw
Dr. Weiner's round eyes. Then I felt her hand softly
stroking mine. "Try to relax."

"What happened?" The shrill ring of her phone
forced her to release my hand. She hung up quickly and
walked back over to the sofa that had the fresh scent of
having just been delivered from the store.

"You fainted. How do you feel?"

"Tired."

"Here are some sleeping pills, samples. They are
very potent. I'm going to have Betty, our receptionist,
drive you home. Call me tomorrow, and I'll make
arrangements for you to meet my partner, Dr. Fowler.
Her training would be better suited to help you."

Betty helped me into her navy-blue sedan and
drove me home. She made sure that I safely entered the
house. After a pill, I lay down on the couch, Sandy's
couch. I picked up the TV remote and turned on the most
mindless thing on television I could find, a daytime talk
show.

I thought about that last therapy session nine years
before. I had become infatuated with Dr. Weiner. After
she had hugged me, I'd locked the office door and kissed
her. She kissed back and pulled me closer. Her body felt
so good against mine, her lips so soft and moist.

She pushed me away. "James, we can't do this."

"What time do you get off work?"

"It's not that. I can't do this with a patient. There
are rules about these things."

"I'm not your patient now. I just graduated."

"I'm worried that you're doing this for the wrong
reasons."

"What? You're intelligent, nurturing and sexy?" I
brushed her soft hair off her forehead.

She turned away. "James, please. I could lose my
license, and I don't think this would be healthy for you

right now." She looked at me. "Maybe after some time passes we can have lunch or something."

I unlocked the door. I had never called.

Light slipped into my half-open eyes. I rose from the couch rubbing my neck, and our cat sat nearby with his tail twitching, wanting his food. The clock read 5:11. I fed the cat, grabbed some bottled water and sat in my chair.

I turned down the TV, and the phone's caller-ID showed that Dr. Weiner called--no call, nothing from the police. I wondered why she had called only a few hours after I had left. Then I realized that I had slept for over twenty hours. Her message expressed concern that my car was still parked near her office. She wanted to know how I was doing. I wasn't sure how I was doing, but I immediately called her and left a voice-mail stating that I was fine.

Perhaps it was the sleep or maybe riding in the backseat of a cab, but I noticed the fresh buds on the oaks and the bright green of the new leaves on the bushes. We turned on Route 28 heading into the heart of Rockville. It was the nice section of town with large homes that offered character and architecture from another time. We passed by a large, red-brick building nestled behind a canopy of large trees. The sign read, Chestnut Lodge Hospital.

The cab dropped me off at my car, and I decided to see if Dr. Weiner might be available. The waiting room was empty. Even Betty was gone. I walked down the hall and heard Dr. Weiner's voice. It sounded strained and quite upset. She slammed down the phone just before I tapped on the half-open door. She turned in alarm.

"Oh, James, you scared me."

"I'm sorry." I looked at the files and pens scattered about her desk. The desk drawers were partially open, and files were strewn about the floor. "I can go--"

"No, it's not you." She stood and grabbed my shoulder. "How do you feel?"

"Better I think. I'm not sure if it was the sleep or just knowing that you're there, here rather."

She picked up her keys and black purse from the desk. "When was the last time you ate?"

"I…"

"Let's go out. I'm famished."

She locked up, and we walked out into a beautiful May evening. The blooms on the flowering pear trees and tulips seemed almost surreal in the dimming light. She seemed like a ghost in her gray pant suit. Her hair lightly tickled the breeze while her heels clicked against the walk.

We walked to a little deli just around the corner and ordered a couple of dinners from a plump waitress with long, red hair tied back in a ponytail. The doughy smell of freshly baked bread sweetened the air. While we sat waiting for our food, Dr. Weiner fiddled with her napkin and stared past me. Her hands moved faster and faster.

"Dr. Weiner?"

"I'm sorry." I had never seen this expression on her face before. It was like being backstage after a play and seeing the actors without their makeup. In this case, her makeup was her professional persona.

"If it's about that pass I made at you back then--"

"It's not you, James."

"I thought you wanted me to kiss you." I leaned toward her.

"I did. That was the problem."

"I'm sorry if I…" I searched her eyes for guidance.

Her professional persona returned. She smiled, but I could sense a distance. "What has been troubling you?"

"What happened in your office yesterday?"

She leaned back. "Do you want to talk about this now?"

I looked down at the blood-red table. "Yes."

"You stood. Your eyes glazed, and you dropped to the floor. Betty and I lifted you onto the sofa, and you started mumbling."

"About what?"

"You kept mumbling something about lions and a woman, Susan, Susan Toller."

I spilled my water, and the glass crashed onto the floor. The ice cubes scurried away in all directions rubbing against the tile floor and sounding like snickering children.

"What's the matter, James?"

The red hair of the waitress swished back and forth as she hurried to the scene of the broken glass. I bent over and started to help her with the broken pieces.

"I'm sorry about that," I said.

She looked up. "Don't worry about it. I got it." She very efficiently collected the pieces of glass and sopped up the water. "Your dinners will be right out." Her hair swished again as she hurried back to the kitchen.

"James, what's wrong?"

"Sandy's been missing for over a week. The cops have been worthless so far." I grabbed my napkin, and Dr. Weiner caressed my hand.

"It's okay. I'm here as a friend," she said.

"I feel responsible. We haven't been getting along lately, and I feel I pushed her away, caused this somehow."

"You shouldn't beat yourself up about this. She might just be out of town for awhile."

"She better have a damn good excuse for putting me through this." I grasped her hand.

The waitress arrived with the food. The plates clattered upon the table, steam rising from both. She replaced my glass of water and put her hands on her broad hips. This gave her the appearance of a two-handled teapot. "You two need anything else?" Now she looked like the warden of the deli.

I looked at Dr. Weiner. "We're fine thank you," I said. The waitress had placed the meals on the wrong sides of the table. I smiled and exchanged her delicious smelling chicken tenderloin for my Salisbury steak. "That smells good."

"Want to try some?" she said.

"Sure." She cut a piece, made sure her fork contained a mushroom and sauce and reached it over to my mouth.

"That's really good. Care for some of mine?"

"Let me see if I can finish this first."

We ate in silence for awhile, and the diner started to fill with the after-happy-hour crowd. I watched the way she placed each bite of food between her moist lips. Then I noticed the rings on her finger. "You're married. You didn't change your last name?"

"Ah. Why change a good therapist name like Weiner? Besides, I'm getting a divorce."

"Is that what's troubling you?"

She finished swallowing some baby carrots. "Christine, my sister, is in the hospital again." She put her fork down for a moment and stared across the room. "I can't help her." Her persona fell away again. "So soon after my brother overdosed." She looked at me. "That's why I was so worried about you yesterday."

"I'm sorry. Is there something I can do?"

"I'll figure something out."

"Hey, doc, you don't have to be perfect all the time. You deserve some help once in awhile too." I winked.

She smiled, and we both started eating again. I changed the subject and talked about the flowers that I planned to plant. We both needed a break from our troubles. She played along and told me some funny office stories. My favorite was the one about the secretary who kept deliberately crashing her computer because she had a crush on the serviceman. Her computer started working fine after he was transferred to Ohio.

She insisted on paying the check, and we walked back to our cars. Dr. Weiner turned as she walked toward hers. "Get some rest and call Dr. Fowler. She is expecting to hear from you."

"Thank you for dinner, Dr. Weiner."

"Call me Robin."

The next day, I found myself on the floor next to the bed, my hip aching. A heavy rain pattered the roof and the windows. After a hot shower, I called the police. The shower failed to quell my fears about Sandy, and the police offered nothing, not even some acting. I tried to return to my writing but ended up listening to the ticks of the second hand on the clock. The seconds passed slowly as if dripping through a clogged water purifier. I missed Sandy's funny way of rubbing her hands and her infectious laugh. I missed me.

The sleeping pills lost their strength, and I started taking two. The same nightmare woke me every night. It was always the same--Sandy lying dead staring up at me. I would try to reach for her, but I couldn't find my hands in the dream, couldn't touch her again. I managed to finish my reading assignments and went downtown to class.

The Metro contained the usual mix of people. It seemed such a contrast to Picketsville, the town near Jefferson College. In front of me stood two black kids wearing baggy jeans and sideways ball caps. Just behind them sat a Hispanic man wearing a crisp olive-tone suit and shiny, black shoes. Next to me sat a young man of Arab descent, and across the isle sat a couple of gabby white girls and an Asian girl using her PDA. Down in Picketsville, when I drove by the Macdonalds, the restaurant and parking lot were filled with black people. There wasn't one white person there. Hardies was where the white kids hung out.

After exiting the Metro, I walked down Massachusetts avenue. A jazz trio was playing nearby and people seemed to have a bounce in their step-- perhaps from the fresh, spring air. The smell of the hotdogs from a vending stand reminded me to eat something, and I quickly choked down a hotdog with mustard and onions.

When I arrived at class, my colleagues expressed their concern regarding my absence. A couple of them asked if they could help in some way, and the professor was very kind. I couldn't figure out how to tell any of them that Sandy was missing without snapping, buckling to my knees. So I didn't.

After class, I took the Metro home. I had to stand due to the number of passengers. I couldn't remember what we had discussed during the second half of class. In fact, I couldn't remember boarding the Metro train. The chime signaling the opening and closing of the train's doors sounded remote as if it were underwater. When I arrived at the Shady Grove stop, the end of the line, my head started to throb with a pulsing pain that blurred my vision. I stumbled into the wire fence that surrounded the parking lot construction work. The sign read METRO with a yellow arrow pointing to the correct rat trail to the

Metro train. Something disturbed me about the sign. I
staggered to my car. It started right up, and I grabbed the
two bucks and a quarter to pay the parking lot attendant. I
was always nice to him, but when I arrived home, I
realized that I had just handed him the money, waited for
the gate to rise and had driven off. I hadn't asked him
about his day as I normally did.

That night, the nightmare came again. Sleep,
despite several pills, failed me for the rest of the night.
The wait for morning seemed endless, but eventually the
birds hailed the rising sun with their melodious chirping.
I heard the cat pawing the bedroom door. I updated his
food and water, told him that I missed Sandy too and
attempted to address the household chores that I had
neglected. The kitchen floor was sticky as well as the
counters, and the dishes were piled up among empty
frozen dinner boxes. The air smelled thick and stale, and I
didn't seem to want to water the drooping plants or eat.

After a few beers and more pills, I still couldn't
sleep. So I raped and murdered a teenage girl. Well, I did
so in the story I was writing. The cat sat on my desk and
inspected the computer screen for grammatical errors and
kept an eye out for any intruders--ants, spiders, bugs.

The pounding on the door startled me. I went
upstairs and cautiously opened the door. A tall fellow
with peppered-gray hair stood on the porch.

"Mr. Douglas? Mr. James Douglas?"

"Yes."

"I'm detective Johnson. May I come in?"

"Okay." He walked in, and I offered him a seat.

He remained stiff and standing. "I'm afraid I have
some bad news."

I sat. "What is it?"

"We found your wife."

I rubbed my knees. "You did?"

"I don't know any other way to say this. We found her body." He unbuttoned his tan blazer.

"Body?" I stood.

He pulled a plastic bag from his shirt pocket. "Do you recognize this?" He held the bag closer.

"That looks like the watch that I gave her for our anniversary." I returned to my chair. "Are you sure?"

"We matched her dental records. Yes."

"What happened?"

"I really can't discuss the case. She was murdered."

"Who? When?"

"Detective Stone has been assigned to the case. He's our best detective. He wanted me to let you know as soon as possible, and he'll be in touch later today or tomorrow. Mr. Douglas…Mr Douglas. Are you okay?"

I looked up. "Would you be?" I wanted to cry to expel the pain but tears even failed me. "Where is she?"

"She's at the Medical Examiner's office in Baltimore."

"I should see her. Are you sure?"

"We're sure. You probably don't want to see her right now. Besides the M.E. is closed now."

I leaned forward and cupped my head in my hands.

"I'm very sorry, Mr. Douglas. Is there anything I can do?"

I looked up. "This Stone character. How do I get in touch with him."

"Here's my card, and I'll write his direct number on the back." He pointed toward the door. "I'll show myself out. I'm sorry Mr. Douglas."

Since Sandy had been missing for so long, I had tried to prepare myself for something like this. I don't know how long I sat there alone with only the cat, our cat. The vast emptiness that I felt changed into rage. Then

the horror of having to call Sandy's mother made me
numb. She picked up after the third ring.

"Margaret, I found Sandy."

"Is she home?"

"She's…"

"What happened?"

"Someone killed her."

"Who…I can't…call you back." I heard the phone
fall and clatter.

"Margaret?" The phone line was dead. I redialed,
but there was no answer. I went upstairs to Sandy's office
and fumbled through the maze of bras and papers
searching for a number for her brother or anyone who
could check on Margaret. With the search unsuccessful, I
returned to the living room and poured a glass of
bourbon. It burned at first but slid down my throat quite
easily after a couple of glasses. The pain pills slid down
one after another. "There's nothing on cable again. I
know there's another bottle here somewhere and more
pills. Seeds always had pills. Ah, Sandy's pain killers for
her teeth. Time for some tunes."

"Hey what are you doing in my living room."

"Can you turn down the music please."

"O'tay."

"I'm Detective Phone."

"Get any calls lately?"

"Please sit down."

"You like Floyd?"

"I'm in charge of your wife's case."

"Pink Floyd. Hey, let's get some mushrooms."

"Please sit down."

"That'd be cool. Have you seen my bong?"

"How many of these pills did you take?"

"It's a glass bong with roses on it. Shit, I busted
it."

"It's empty."

"I need a refill. Let's have a shot?"

"Give me that bottle. I'm the police."

"I'll get you a glass. Fuck it. Use mine. I'll just drink from the bottle. Oops, we may need a new one soon."

"You need to come with me."

"We can just pour the rest of this in the bong. Got JD and Wiiiild Turkey, gobble gobble."

"I'm serious."

"Me too telephone man. Hey, my phone in the kitchen's been kind of wacky--"

"Don't make me--"

"Oh man, this is 'The Crunge,' great tune, used to play it in my band, five-four time, tricky stuff. Let's finish the tune, and then we can go get those shrooms. Put on some tunes, Hip. Seeds and Stems, that's what they used to call us. Seeds stole pills from his Dad, a shrink. We crushed them up and sprinkled the Darvon, Demorol, Ritalin and Valium into the weed--no seeds or stems though. Hey nice car. We should probably wash it. Then he ripped off some liquid Demorol and a bunch of needles. We were almost too fucked up to take a bong hit after we injected that into our arm or leg. Nobody wanted to change the album, too lazy. Pretty cool. We going to get those shrooms. Sorry I broke the bong. Cruzin, yeah. Cool lights. What's the name of this tune?"

"Siren."

Sandy is just lying there, blood trickling from her nose, her soft, brown hair tangled on the dewy grass. Her eyes stare at the sky. A large, black ant crawls down her nose. Her clothes are torn, and her right hand is clenched into a fist. Her legs are now bent as if kneeling before falling back into the moist blades of grass. Her white stockings are torn and stained green...almost yellow. She

turns her eyes toward me, and her left hand raises her
car keys. "Why," her lips mouth.

Slowly, light crept into my eyes. The room was
bright, and smelled of rubbing alcohol and bleach.
Various machines blinked green or red screens, and I
noticed an IV in my arm. I tried to call out and found
only excruciating pain. A blurry, white apparition came
into the room and said, "nice to see you awake." It stuck a
thermometer in my mouth, did something with the IV and
the various machines. "I'll go get the doctor."

He came in along with a girl. His balding head
and bushy, gray eyebrows slowly sharpened into view.
With her petite hand, the girl removed the thermometer,
blinked her innocent, green eyes and offered an attempt at
a reassuring smile.

"You gave us quite a scare," he said. "Don't try to
speak yet. Just nod for now, okay?" He spoke with a
slight British accent.

I nodded. His firm, thin fingers poked around my
abdomen and my throat which felt raw and swollen. Then
he shone a small flashlight into my eyes. He smiled and
asked many questions regarding my condition. I certainly
didn't understand the nature of my condition, and I was
very unclear regarding where I was.

"You seem fine, Mr. Douglas."

I frowned at him. I didn't feel fine. My stomach
and throat felt as if a horse were standing on me. My
mouth was parched and my eyes dry.

"You are at Shady Grove Hospital. Detective
Stone brought you in last night." He fiddled with the
instruments in his white smock pocket. "Given his war
injury, it must have been a real chore for him to bring you
here." He picked up my chart. "You were delirious when
he found you, and given the combination of the pain
killers and alcohol, you may just owe him your life." He
returned the chart to the foot of the bed. "You can

probably go home tomorrow, but you need some more rest." I nodded. "We have a specialist that I would like you to speak with in a few days regarding your attempted suicide."

I frantically motioned for paper and pen, and I scribbled Dr. Robin Weiner's name and phone number. The green-eyed nurse removed the IV.

The next day, a girl wearing a bright red shirt with a bluish patch brought me some magazines, and I caught up on the world's chaos. All the covers of the magazines pictured a senator who was embroiled in some sex scandal or an airbrushed photo of a woman with threateningly large breasts. Nuclear holocaust in the eastern hemisphere would have been buried at the end of the rags along with the ads for psychics and ex-presidents' memoirs. She returned with some water. She was somewhat heavy with cropped black hair and a small nose beneath gray-green eyes. She sat next to the bed. I pointed to the patch on her shirt.

"Oh, I'm a volunteer." She placed the straw into my mouth. "The nurse said I should tell you to try to talk, but just a little." She pulled back the straw.

I choked. "Why volunteer?"

She looked away. "My therapist suggested it."

I touched her hand and smiled. It felt soft and a bit sweaty. "Glad you're here."

She smiled. "Overeating. I over eat."

"There are far worse things." I smiled. She returned the straw to my mouth.

Robin entered the room wearing a burgundy pant suit which accentuated her narrow waist in contrast to her breasts and hips. She touched the volunteer's shoulder. "May I?"

The volunteer handed the water glass to her. "Slowly." She left.

Robin sat next to the bed. "How are you feeling?"
She stroked my arm.

I sat up a bit. "I'm sorry for--"

"No. I'm sorry." She looked down at the bed. "I
should have seen this coming. The important thing is that
you are all right."

We sat for awhile in silence. Her hand on my arm
told me everything I wanted to know. I picked up a
magazine and flipped to a cartoon that I liked, a
publishing agent dressed as a vampire. Robin's full lips
curled upward.

"Are you ready to go home?" she asked.

"Yes," I said with a raspy voice. My stomach
growled.

The volunteer helped me into the wheelchair, and
then Robin helped me into her silver Lexus. We picked
up some fast food along the way. The chocolate
milkshake really helped. We arrived at my townhouse,
and she helped me in the door. The cat greeted us and
then complained about his growling stomach.

"Where's her food?" Robin asked after seeing me
to the couch. I told her, and she fed him. She returned to
the living room. "Cute cat."

"He's in charge of security here."

Robin sat next to me on the couch and unwrapped
my burger for me. "The doctor told me to get some food
into you."

"Yes'm."

"This is a nice place, James. I suppose you read a
lot." She took a bite of her chicken sandwich.

"It's a new hobby for me. It's not as well
organized as I would like." I started pointing my burger
around the room. "History there, modern and post modern
literature there, Greek, Roman, Medieval sections,
computer science, math there. Behind us are the how-to
books on writing and that voodoo science of psychiatry."

31

She grinned. "Well, a sense of humor is a good sign."

I pointed across the pine table. "That's the reference section and current reading for this semester." I nibbled at the burger.

She finished her sandwich. "What provoked you to pursue writing?"

"Seemed like the fastest way to become poor."

"Exactly. The James I knew nine years ago wore pin-striped suits and was going to conquer the computer industry."

"I suppose I started to feel like an empty suit. I have much newer and nicer suits now if you would like to see them." I dropped half the burger back onto the wrapper.

"No. I've always liked the artistic side of you, except for the overdose part." Her speech accelerated. "James, I can take you over to Chestnut Lodge for a few days. They'll--"

"I'm fine." I stood and paused. "I'm sorry I snapped at you." I picked up the fast food leftovers and trash. "Looks like I owe you two dinners now. Let me cook you dinner. We can discuss Jung and Erikson. I'll have to study a bit to keep up."

"No Freud?" She picked up her purse.

"Must have been a slip."

"Are you sure you will be all right?"

"If you say yes to dinner."

"Yes, maybe in a few days, but I will call tomorrow to make sure that you are all right." She stood and caressed my cheek. I so much wanted to kiss her, but felt weak and dirty. After she left, I threw out the leftovers and lay on the couch.

The next day, the doorbell rang during the mid-afternoon. I opened the door expecting a solicitor, or worse, two young men holding *Bibles*. A frightening looking fellow with a round, pocked face, hollow eyes and a hunched stance greeted me. His black and gray hair rustled in the summer breeze.

"Good afternoon, Mr. Douglas. I'm Detective Stone. May I have a word with you?" A couple of kids ran by the house yelling.

"Of course. I assume this is about my wife?" He nodded. Then he walked with a strange limp through the small foyer and up three steps to the living room dragging his right leg as if it refused to be lifted. I waved my hand toward the loveseat, and he sat down. The black leather released a crunching sound. "I was about to make some coffee?"

"I'm fine. This won't take long," Stone said.

I sat down. "Any luck?"

"We're pursuing every lead. We think she was killed on June thirteenth." He plucked a cigarette out of his yellow shirt pocket. "It appears that she went to work by Metro, and when she walked to her car at the Shady Grove stop that night, she was dragged into the nearby brush and killed."

I stood and handed him a ceramic ashtray. "Those damn lights have been out due to the construction there."

His eyes were dark, expressionless. His face seemed to sag in a permanent frown. "Have any matches?" I went to the kitchen, and when I returned with a book of matches, Stone was leaning over the library table thumbing through my research notes. Tan threads of his blazer dangled over his wrinkled, blue slacks. I handed him the matches. "So, you're familiar with the Metro?"

"Yes."

"Where were you that night, Mr. Douglas?" He wandered around the room examining my books.

"The thirteenth?"

He turned. "It was a Wednesday." White smoke curled out of his nose.

"I would have been right here studying."

"Alone?"

"Yes," I said.

"What do you do for a living?" He flicked an ash into the ashtray.

"I sell computer products, but I've taken a break from that to work on a graduate degree in writing." We both sat back down.

"How were you and your wife getting along?" Stone asked.

"We didn't see much of each other. She arrived home from work late during the week, and I spent most of my weekends writing or doing research out of town." I started rubbing the arms of the black leather chair.

"Where?"

"Jefferson College. It's near Lynchburg."

Stone put out his cigarette. "When was the last time you saw your wife?"

"Probably the night before."

"I need to have a look at her things."

I showed him the upstairs. He turned, handed me a search warrant and said, "I won't be long." I took the hint and went back down the stairs to pour a glass of water. My mouth was unusually dry. The back of my neck and forehead were moist with sweat. Washing the dishes offered a slight distraction from the realization that I might be a suspect. While I was wiping down the counters, Stone came down the stairs. I dried my hands and walked into the living room. He probed some more about my relationship with Sandy and about my whereabouts. Stone held up a clear plastic bag.

"I'm taking a few of her things for the investigation."

"Of course." We concluded with my assurance that I wasn't leaving town, and I gave him the location and schedule of my classes.

He handed me his card. "Here's the number of a crisis hotline if you need to talk to someone. It works better than swallowing a bottle of pills." He wrote it on the back of the card. "If you think of anything, give me a call. I'll be in touch."

He let himself out. I locked the door behind him and placed the card on the pine coffee table. I sat, flipped on the TV and picked up the TV Guide. My thoughts became disjointed as if the fragments of Greek plays--a character here, a story there, all incomplete, burned by Romans. I put the food-fight news show on mute. D.C. seemed so far away. I stood and started to reorganize the books on the shelves around me. I became frustrated trying to separate the modern and post modern writers. There appeared to be no clear line of demarcation. I went to the refrigerator which smelled of leftover delivery food and popped a beer. I leaned against the white counter and gazed into the dining room which was essentially part of both the living room and kitchen--all one large room separated only by a closet near the center. I first polished the light-oak hardwood floors in the living room and dining room. Next, I scrubbed the paisley-blue floor tile in the foyer and kitchen. Due to the nine foot ceiling, I had to use a ladder to completely polish the light-oak cabinets in the kitchen. My footing became unsteady due to the increasing amount of beer in my system. My rambling thoughts began to calm, and I sat down with a fresh beer and a note pad. I gazed at my expensive stereo and wondered when I had last listened to Mozart or plugged my Fender into the sound mixer to jam along with Roy Buchanan or Foghat. I turned up the sound on the TV and began cleaning the beer from the refrigerator one at a time. Fantasies of Robin interfered with the TV. I thought about that one kiss we had shared. I thought about her in various colors of lingerie, how good she tasted. I staggered up the stairs to bed and pulled the pillows close.

The Lion is sitting on the bed. "Come here and scratch behind my ears," he says.

"Do you have a name?"

"You already know." He purrs and pats my shoulder with his paw, his claws extending and retracting. The roof of the bedroom rips away, and a torrent of clouds swirl while the air evaporates.

I hear the slap from upstairs and mother thumping onto the floor...again. Steve is cuddled up in his box. He's crying.

The yelling, every night, the yelling, the thumps above us. Father's footsteps on the stairs pound against my ears. Steve closes his box.

"I can't..."

"I know." The Lion's fur feels warm against my skin. His purring grows louder. I'm watching myself dream. His purring softens. I can't feel him now.

Two days later, Stone left a voice mail that they were done with Sandy's body. I phoned Sandy's mother and asked if I should render any specific instructions regarding the funeral. She said that she was not able to help financially but that she would appreciate it if a Catholic priest performed the ceremony.

"I'll take care of it," I said. "I was thinking this Sunday?"

"What happened?"

"The police are still investigating."

"Why didn't you protect her?"

"I...I'll call you later regarding the funeral." I hung up. She was right. I should have protected Sandy.

I chose a nearby cemetery in Germantown and a closed-casket ceremony. The detectives recommended that I not see the body. The bulk of the money went toward the casket and the floral arrangements. I declined the limousine service or some form of reception after we put Sandy in the ground. Robin offered to attend, but we agreed that her presence might be inappropriate. She insisted on seeing me afterward. So I gave her a key to my townhouse to wait for me.

The funeral was brief. A warm, June rain darkened the red clay around Sandy's grave. The Catholic priest mumbled some allegedly prophetic words. Her mother wept, and I stood holding a black umbrella over her. Sandy's brother stood wearing a cheap, brown blazer and black slacks, and he held a blue umbrella over his sister who, like her mother, wore a black dress. It was the first time I met them, and I avoided their cold, accusing glares. The other sister was out of the country and could not attend.

I placed a pink rose, Sandy's favorite, on the casket and walked her mother to her car. She said nothing. I had no idea what I could say. I had lost a wife. She had lost her daughter. After I closed the door, Sandy's brother bumped into me. "I'll be in touch," he said.

I drove through the slanting sheets of rain and filmy puffs of steam rising from the gray asphalt. Knowing that Robin was there waiting steadied my resolve to move through this event, the first of its kind in my life after we had buried my father and little brother.

The cat greeted me at the garage door. I slipped off my wet shoes and stroked his orange fur. He scurried up the stairs ahead of me. Robin was standing in the living room wearing blue jeans and a green polo shirt. I looked away and went into the kitchen for some water.

She followed. "James, I know you have no one else."

"Is that what I am to you, a charity case?" I grabbed the counter and squeezed until the edges formed lines in my palms. I turned around. "Basket case, something for your research perhaps?"

"James, please--"

"Maybe you should put me in a cage and study me, doc." She left the kitchen. I waved my arm across the counter smashing the spices and knife racks against the walls. The pasta holder, Sandy's pasta holder, shattered into the sink.

I opened a bottle of wine and grabbed two glasses along with a bottle of aspirin. I set a glass on the coffee table in front of Robin and filled hers, then mine. "I'm sorry, Robin." I handed her the wine glass. "Thank you for being here."

"I didn't mean--"

"I know." I sat next to her on the couch.

She sipped her wine. "I brought some sandwiches from the deli. You should eat."

I refilled my glass. "She's gone now."

"I'm sorry."

"Sandwiches?"

"I'm here, James." She stroked my neck.

"This was her couch."

"Yes."

"I'm afraid."

I awoke on the couch and found my charcoal-colored suit coat draped over the back of it and my red tie loosened. The cat was clearly hungry, and after changing into some jeans, I drove to the vet to buy some more food for him. He could only eat special food. It was hard to resist giving him table scraps that would probably kill him. Every day and night, he ate the same food--like you or I eating tuna fish every night for dinner. They have his records in the computer at the vet's. I asked the young lady to pull up Oliver McConnell.

"Nothing," she turned, her long black hair wrapping around her neck. "Nothing for Oliver McConnell."

"Try Oliver Douglas."

She found his computer file, and I bought his food. I had played a small joke on Sandy soon after we married. We had gone back and forth about her last name, and in somewhat of a joke I had told her that her last name was Douglas...period. She changed her name. Shortly afterward, she went to the vet to buy some food for Oliver and discovered that I had changed his last name too. It was funny at the time.

I drove home, and after feeding the cat, I called Robin and apologized for my behavior. I later discovered that the cat was upset about his litter. He left the subtle message of a few turds next to his litter box in the office. Throughout the week, I began to realize how many of the household chores Sandy had performed--washing the bath towels, cleaning the bathrooms, changing the litter. Robin and I spoke every evening over the phone. She served as the only anchor in what had become a very confusing existence.

The following week, I invited Robin over for dinner to thank her for her help. She accepted. That Saturday, I went to the store and picked out the best peppers, scallions, garlic and chicken breasts. I called a business friend in Boulder who knew something about wine, and upon his advise, I bought two very expensive bottles. Back at home, I stood in the walk-in closet trying to decide what to wear. None of my jeans seemed to fit the way I wanted, and I must have tried on half a dozen shirts. It took me ten minutes to decide to wear some cologne which I don't normally wear at all. She arrived promptly, came through the unlocked door, and her heels clicked on the oak steps.

I walked over to her. "Please forgive my behavior the other day."

She said nothing and smiled. She cupped her hand around the back of my neck and pulled my lips to hers. I wrapped my arms around her and gently kissed back. Her waist felt firm, and her breasts warm against my chest. Soon her tongue was dueling with mine. Her hands rubbed my back while my hands explored her hips and her sexy ass. She released me.

"I assume the bedroom is upstairs?" She removed her black heels and started up the stairs. I followed. I looked at my hands to assure myself that I was not dreaming. In the bedroom, Robin quickly removed the clothes that I had labored over, and I kissed her while unzipping her black skirt which glided down her black, thigh-high stockings. She removed her white blouse and then her bra. I licked her erect nipples until she guided my mouth lower. Then she pulled me into the bed and straddled me, her thighs against my cheeks. She remained there for quite some time while I employed every trick I knew. "Yes, just like that, James." She shuddered, let out a deep moan and rolled off of me. She ran her nails along my stomach and my aching erection. "We'll take care of this a little later. That felt good."

I stood and grabbed a green bath towel and wiped off my face and then her thighs. "Hungry?"

"Very."

"Would you like to relax in the hot tub while I cook?"

"That sounds perfect."

I filled the tub while she rolled her stockings down her firm, slender legs. I showed her how to adjust the jets and lay my blue bathrobe on the sink. She kissed me. "I know you like being teased."

I grinned going down the stairs. I did like being teased, but perhaps my smile derived more from pleasing her than anything else. Then again, it may have been my fantasies about what we would do to each other after dinner.

I carefully placed the seasoned and flowered chicken breasts into the sizzling olive oil and browning garlic. Then, I mixed in the sliced green, yellow and red peppers. I flavored the linguini, dab of butter, squeeze of freshly sliced lemon, a sprinkle, two, of basil and poured a bit of wine over the chicken and peppers. I opened the oven, and the sweet aroma from the French bread hovered over the kitchen and dining room. Robin walked into the kitchen wearing one of my blue, button-down dress shirts. I promptly pulled out a chair for her and filled our wine glasses. I filled our plates as artistically as possible and then grated a wedge of parmesan cheese over the linguini, chicken and peppers.

"This is delicious, James."

"Thank you. More wine?"

"Please. I could get used to this."

"Good."

After dinner, I left the dishes, and we sat in the living room with the wine. After Vivaldi finished illustrating the seasons, I led her upstairs. She very quickly released the tension in my shorts. I lay my head between her breasts and caressed her hip while she played with my hair.

I woke to the chirping birds and the sunlight dimmed by the midnight-blue curtains. The characters of my novel had filled my dreams, demanding attention, consuming my internal dialogue, each a fragment of myself--arguing, fearing, loving, philosophizing, living.

After I sat up, I saw a pair of black panties on the pillow and knew that Robin was more than a dream.

The kitchen was clean, and the cat curled around my legs until I updated his food and water. I started the coffee maker which gurgled, sounding like the sound effects of some alien in a cult, black and white science fiction movie.

After his meal, the cat helped with editing, and I poured out page after page of the story. His orange fur on my manuscript didn't bother me. Each sentence flowed without hesitation, without pause. I didn't have to plan anything. It just poured through my fingers onto the keyboard. Time that had ticked so slowly before dissipated into the air like water poured onto a hot desert stone, and it was soon almost dinner time, time to call Robin. The doorbell rang. I walked from my office, up the stairs and opened the door, hoping it was Robin. I opened the door and the deathly cold eyes of Detective Stone met mine.

"Detective Stone?"

"May I come in?" I further opened the door and waved my arm. He sat on the loveseat again.

"The reason I'm here…" He adjusted his black slacks.

"Yes." I walked toward my chair.

"I'll take you up on that coffee from last time."

"Of course." I went into the kitchen and started the coffee maker. Upon my return, Stone was flipping through my manuscript.

He looked up. "So, you are a writer?"

"Depends on your definition." The science fiction alien sound effects gurgled nearby.

"What's your story about?" he said as he limped back to the loveseat.

"Not sure yet."

"I know this is hard, but do you know a Kevin Brown?"

"Kevin Brown...no."

"We think he killed her, and we have him in custody."

"Why?" I looked across the room at my acoustic guitar that sorely needed new strings. "I'll get that coffee for you."

"You don't know him?"

"No." I went to the kitchen and returned with two cups.

He sipped his coffee. "They were having an affair."

I set my cup down. "How long?"

"I can't discuss details at this time."

"How long?"

"For awhile." I sipped his coffee but kept staring at me.

"Are you sure?"

"I'm sure. You don't know him?"

"No. I told you that already."

He awkwardly stood, thanked me for the coffee and started limping down the stairs.

"I'll be in touch." Then he turned his hunched shoulders around, pulled a pack of smokes out of his pale-green shirt pocket, removed one and started to tap the butt against his thumbnail. "Strange thing." He placed the cigarette in his mouth which drooped from his sagging lips. "Her cell phone records show that she called here that night, the night she was probably killed."

I grabbed the oak banister next to the foyer stairs. "Yes?"

"It was shortly before we think she was murdered. Did you speak with her that night?"

"I..." He twitched the unlit cigarette in a circle with his frowning lips. "Don't think so. I would remember that."

He sparked a wooden match and exhaled through his flattened nose. "Good luck with your story."

No Quarter

I didn't see the Fourth of July fireworks. I wrote.
Robin came by every couple of days. She of course
continued to dominate our sexual sessions, but I liked
that. I cooked for her every time that she came over and
learned new recipes just for her. She liked Italian which
can be relatively simple, and I learned how to cook a few
German dishes.

"This hot potato salad is great." Her fork clicked
against the plate.

"Not too much vinegar?"

"Maybe less pepper."

"Yes, I'm developing a pepper problem. Think I
should call a shrink?"

She laughed while cutting another piece of the
chicken strudel. She continued to smile. "Have you called
Dr. Fowler yet?"

I ground more black pepper over my plate and
noticed my hands shaking. "Is the wine okay?"

"Fine." The wicker seat crunched as she delicately
crossed her legs.

She was only wearing one of my white dress
shirts which shifted colors among white, gray and
sometimes yellow in the flickering candle light. Her hair
was a bit messy, and part of her bangs rested on her
narrow eyebrows. I glanced at my plate just long enough
to secure a bite of food to my fork, and the rest of the
time my eyes scanned Robin's round face and smooth
thighs. She ate the chicken strudel and the tomatoes
covered with basil and Italian dressing as if someone
were going to steal them from her. A Mozart violin
concerto softly caressed the pauses of conversation.

"There's plenty more," I said.

"Yes, please, more of everything." She handed me
her plate.

I stepped a few feet to the counter. She stroked my arm as I set another serving in front of her. I topped off her glass of wine, gently brushed her hair off her forehead with my fingers and kissed her warm cheek. I sat back down adjacent to her. "Well, you do seem to enjoy my cooking."

"It's great, but orgasms always make me hungry."

"So, you're not sure if it's the cooking or the sex?"

"Does it matter?"

I cut another piece of strudel. "Good point."

"James, you've hardly touched your food."

"I...you know I'm crazy about you." That was the same thing I had said to Sandy when we first started dating. Robin was sitting in the same chair in which Sandy used to sit. A feeling of guilt swept through me. I simply could not stop thinking about Robin. The sex was terrific, but there was much more. She knew me better than anyone--my faults, my failures, my desires. There were things about me that only she and I knew--like my cocaine abuse and being beaten up by two, large, black girls when I was in eighth grade. I could tell her anything. I guarded my checkered past and emotions from most people. She was provocative and yet professional, both nurturing and stern. When she was near me, all I could think about was holding her. When we were apart, which seemed far too often, I longed for her soothing and melodic voice.

She finished eating, put her fork down and then looked at me. "James, I need to know if you are okay. It's important." She took a sip of wine. "Please call Dr. Fowler."

For a brief moment I could see only her round face floating in the dark background. I smiled and winked both my eyes. "I'll call her." She smiled back, and we then raised our glasses in a silent toast.

It was an unusually cool night for August. "Let me help you with the dishes," she said.

I wouldn't let her help. "That CD is almost over." After I cleared the table, I heard classical guitar music. I loaded the dishwasher while struggling to remember the artist's name. I found Robin on the couch in the living room flipping through my manuscript, handed her a fresh glass of wine and set some cookies on the coffee table.

"Thank you," she said as I sat down next to her.

"You know if you wear a man's dress shirt without a tie, you shouldn't button it up so high." I rubbed her tan thigh.

She fiddled with the buttons. "How is school going?"

"Good. They're keeping me busy."

"That's probably good for you right now." She pinched my nipple.

"Ouch." She pulled the partially buttoned shirt over her head, then slid my shorts off and placed her open lips against mine.

Sweaty, naked and panting, we held each other afterward. I stroked her thick hair while she gently ran her nails back and forth along my thighs. I kissed the top of her head.

The cat sat next to the couch, patiently waiting to request his food. I stood and noticed that the deck door and living room windows were still open and wondered how many of the neighbors had heard us. I felt confident that they must have heard Robin's moans and the sexy, domineering way she had spoken to me. I fed the cat, and given the falling temperature, went upstairs and retrieved a bathrobe for Robin and some jeans and a tee shirt for me.

She sat twirling a lock of hair with her fingers. I draped the robe over her bare shoulders. "Is this all right?" Her fingers tangled her hair more frantically.

Then I noticed a glistening in her lovely eyes. My arm
instinctively extended toward her, "what--"

"I can't help her." She pulled the robe tight around
her.

"Robin?"

She picked up a cookie.

"What are you talking about?"

She dropped the cookie back into the box and
handed me her empty wine glass. "Christine needs better
help with her condition."

"What's wrong with her?"

"I just treat compulsive behavior, eating disorders
mostly. She's had some form of psychotic break with
reality. I can't reach her." She squeezed my arm and
looked up at me from the couch. I couldn't stand to see
tears on her cheeks or the pain in her eyes. Her voice had
moved between rage and anguish.

"I'll get the wine."

When I returned, she was dabbing her eyes with
purple tissues. She looked down at her naked feet. "I'm
sorry. I know--"

"Don't worry about it." I handed her a full glass of
wine and sat next to her. "We'll be fine. I love you."

She quickly stood. The wine and glass slipped
from her hand and splattered on the hardwood floor. She
ran upstairs, and a sharp pain piercing my left foot halted
my attempt to follow. I fell back onto the couch. The cat
ran down the stairs to the basement. Blood drizzled from
my foot as I tried to remove the glass, and my blood
joined the wine on the hardwood floor. I had said the
three most dangerous words in the English language.
They just popped out without thought, without hesitation
and without warning. Robin came back down the steps
with her clothes and headed for the door. She paused with
her back to me.

"James, I care about you too. It's just that I'm still married."

"Robin, please don't go. Let me help."

She set her purse down and slipped on her panties, skirt and blouse. "It's more complicated than you know." She picked up her purse and partially stuffed her bra and stockings into it.

"Would you turn on that light?" I couldn't see the glass in the candle light. She turned on the foyer light and saw me holding my foot.

"James?"

"Careful of the glass."

She dropped her purse. "Where's the first aid kit?" I told her where it was in the kitchen, and she promptly returned with it and a towel. I slid down the couch away from the glass.

"This is a great deal of blood. Maybe I should drive you to the emergency room." I shook my head. She wiped the blood off my foot and with the blue plastic tweezers from the kit, pulled out the shard of glass. Despite my efforts to conceal the pain, a small yelp expelled from my mouth. The antiseptic didn't improve my disposition.

"Maybe I should serve you wine in a plastic cup next time." I smiled.

"I'm sorry," she said. "You surprised me." She bandaged my foot and then wiped up the wine, glass and blood. "We just need to take this slowly. There are things you don't know, and I can't discuss them right now. Please understand."

"When can I see you again?"

"Soon." She ran her fingers through my hair and kissed my forehead. "I have to go before Reginald gets home." She turned off the light and left.

Hobbling like the detective who had saved my life, I locked the front door and then limped into the dining room. The candles on the table waved against my breath and flickered out. The CD clicked off. The living room was lit only by the stripes of light peeking through the blinds from the street lamp. I fumbled through the CD's. Nothing seemed appropriate. I picked up the white stocking that Robin had dropped in her hurry to leave and sat on the couch in the dark, kneading it between my fingers and thumb. The silence was deafening.

Upstairs, I could smell Robin's perfume on my pillow and wondered if my friend the Lion would come again tonight. Sleep slithered in and out of my grasp for what may have been only minutes or hours, but eventually I held onto it long enough to dream.

Francis lives in the woods in a shack next to our horse pasture. He's black and wears a funny hat. My little brother, Steve, wants to see him. So Steve and me creep up the side of the pasture along the wire fence that my cousin, Dad and me put up. I tell Steve that Francis is dangerous, and we need to be really quiet. Steve wants to see him though.

I can hardly keep quiet when Steve steps in some horse manure. He wipes his black tennis shoe on the grass while I cup my hand over my mouth. That's one of my jobs, spreading horse manure around the pasture to fertilize the grass. We keep going along the fence, next to the woods.

I point into the woods. "Right there was a yellow jacket nest. See that hole? I burned 'em up with kerosene. Dad wore a big net on his face, but I didn't need one. I just poured it in and threw in a match and ran."

"Are we gettin' close?"

"Yeah. Be real quiet."

We reach the top of the hill next to the shack and hide behind a big oak tree and watch to see if Francis will come out. Steve looks scared.

"He's got a big ax," I say real quiet like. "And he's always talking to the trees or something,"
"Is that him?" Steve points.
"Yeah, quiet," I whisper.
Francis the Ax Man comes walking around the shack wiggling his hands. "Got's to get this furniture out the yard. Damn bottles. Francis got's trees though, 'cept Francis hates them squirrels...be stealin'."
"Where's his ax," Steve whispers.
"He only gets it out when he wants to kill somebody."
Francis stops and fiddles with his gray hat. I raise my finger to my mouth to hush Steve. A squirrel runs by and Steve jumps up.
"Who dat," says Francis. Steve runs down the hill, slips on some horse manure and falls. I laugh, but Francis hears me.
"You boys leave ole Francis be...scat...git out here. Damn squirrels."
I run after Steve. I can outrun him, but he's really moving. I catch up at the bottom where my pony once threw me.
The boxes are still in my way. The yellow monsters swoop down as the sky crumbles into bits of stars. Steve lies still in the grass--no yellow jackets now. The Lion swishes his tail against the bridge, and I hear Susan's cry.
The Lion is curled up in the corner again. Susan hands me the soap. My arms cannot reach. I try. The soap clatters on the shower floor. The door steams. It is dark now. I struggle into a pair of jeans, throw on a sweatshirt and step into the hallway. The Lion is gone now. The air is cold.

She didn't return my calls to her office. Of course, I couldn't really call Robin's house because of her soon-to-be ex-husband, and I spent a few days accomplishing absolutely nothing. I finally managed to return to my novel. The murders were becoming more violent. The character's frustration increased with each act, and each act needed to be more dramatic. While I was brutally murdering another girl, the doorbell rang in a frantic fashion. I cautiously opened the front door. Robin barreled through with a small girl in her arms. She bound up the stairs and set the little girl on the couch. The little girl wore a cute, peach-colored dress and seemed very confused and disoriented, like me.

Robin turned around. "That bastard isn't going to get away with this." Then, I noticed the swelling under her eye--her partially closed, black and blue eye. My affection and confusion quelled the rage swelling within me.

I closed the door and walked over to her. "Robin, let me help." She turned away.

The little girl on the couch fidgeted with her hair and dress. Her head hung toward the floor. Robin wandered into the kitchen. I didn't have any idea what to do. I picked up the TV Guide and found a cartoon channel and turned it on. I moved a jar of hard candy over to the little girl and noticed a green stain on her dress.

"These are my favorite," I said. She took one. I cautiously ventured into the kitchen and approached Robin. I looked at her swollen eye.

"I'll get some ice," I said. I grabbed the ice pack that I used for my back and escorted her up the stairs. She accepted the ice pack and raised the comforter to cover all but her face.

"Can I get you a drink?"

"Her name is Cynthia." She looked at me with her uncovered eye. "Can you look after her for awhile?"

"Yes, just get some rest now."

Downstairs, I had no idea what to do with a little
girl. Grown women were difficult enough. But, there sat
a five-year-old girl sucking on a cherry Life Saver staring
at her feet instead of grinning at Elmer Fudd. I fed the cat
and realized how little food there was in the house.
I took Cynthia to the store to buy us all some
food. I attempted the usual questions. I asked about her
age, if she was in school, her favorite candy, anything I
could think of. She didn't want to talk. I didn't blame her.
Who was I to her?

"I have a cat."

"Is he nice?" She looked up while we walked
through the frozen food section. A clerk dropped a crate
of canned goods. The crash nearly made me drop the
shopping basket. Cynthia's tiny hand reached up to mine.

"I think he'd like you."

That was the first time I saw her smile. "Can we
have barb-a-cue chicken?"

"Absolutely." Convincing her to look to me for
protection felt like some major achievement, and I found
myself naturally protective of her. We left with the
chicken breasts, some chocolate bars, 'tater salad (as she
called it), and I drove to the nearby liquor store. I parked
where I could keep an eye on her while she waited in the
car. I wasn't sure which frightened me more--telling
Robin that I took this little girl into a liquor store or that I
left her in the car. Cynthia was into the chocolate bars
when I arrived with the brandy and wine. She was upset
when I took away the candy and she tried unsuccessfully
to stomp her feet which couldn't reach the floorboard.

My hands felt clammy, and I could hear my
father's voice scolding me for not mowing the lawn.
Then I remembered the ice wrapped in a towel that
Mother used to give me afterward.

"Mister?" We were still sitting in the lot, the
chocolate melting. She fiddled with her ponytail and

seemed understandably worried. So was I. I wasn't sure how long we had been sitting there. "Is Aunty okay?" My twitching hand fumbled to get the key into the ignition.

"I think so, yes."

"I'm sorry I made you mad."

"You didn't...barbecue chicken coming up." She twirled a lock of her brown hair around her finger. "Put on your seatbelt please."

She struggled with it until I helped her. Her knees were red, almost bruised, and her hair fell from her ponytail. "You're not going to do anything bad to me are you?"

"Of course not." She had me wrapped around her little finger--nothing I could do about it. When we walked up through the garage entrance, Robin was sitting on the couch. She held the ice pack against the left side of her face. Cynthia ran over and hugged her leg. Then they watched cartoons while I grilled the chicken out on the deck. I wondered why I had taken the chocolate away from Cynthia. It had seemed like some form of automatic reflex.

I covered the grill and went inside to check on them. "Do you need a fresh ice pack?"

"Please." Robin smiled and handed me the pack. I soon returned with a colder one. The cat came down from his closet and immediately jumped up on the couch and cuddled up to Robin. Cynthia, of course, wanted to pet him. He ran away having never been around a child.

Back on the deck, I flipped the chicken. The gray and white stray cat that I always see around twilight slunk along the neighbor's fence, and an intermittent breeze fanned the flames of the grill.

"About five minutes until dinner," I said through the door opening.

"We get chocolate after the chicken," Cynthia told Robin.

Dinner went as well as one could hope, but Cynthia objected to the green peppers that I had grilled with the chicken. Robin removed them from Cynthia's plate. Cynthia finished her chicken and 'tater salad before Robin and me. Robin stared across the room at nothing, and I stared at her wondering what I could do, what had happened. Cynthia waited patiently, swinging her tiny legs under the table, occasionally clicking her shoes against the chair rungs. Robin said nothing and seemed to be hungry only for the wine. Cynthia and I waited for Robin to quit picking at her food, and I cleared the table while Cynthia requested some chocolate. I pointed to chocolate bars, and Robin handed one to Cynthia.

I finished the dishes and heard the channels change and Cynthia's giggle from the living room. I left them alone--seemed best. After cleaning up the bedroom and starting a load of laundry, I poured a couple of brandies and found Robin and Cynthia sleeping on the couch.

I wandered onto the deck still holding both brandies. My new neighbor was on his deck, smoking a cigar.

"Welcome to the neighborhood. I'm James."

He introduced himself as Mark and reached his hand over to shake. My hands full, I handed a brandy over to him. He swirled the butt of his cigar in it.

"Thanks man. Been a tough week."

I looked up at the sky. "Cool moon."

"Peach."

"What?"

"It's a peach-moon." He sipped the brandy.

I gazed up at a hazy, peach-colored moon. "Waxing gibbous you think?"

"A who?"

"Waxing gibbous, it could be waning--not sure really--might be full."

"Good brandy." He took another sip.

"Have plenty."

"Peach-moon. That's rare. Only seen one before."
His black hair quivered in the August breeze. He handed
the glass back to me, and I quickly returned with the
bottle after turning down the TV. The cat cautiously
walked out on the deck with me and rendered a soft
meow as he did when he was out there hunting in his
little world.

"Your cat?" he asked.

"Yes. Any bugs out here are in serious trouble."

He leaned closer over his deck rail. "Heard you
two going at it the other day. Sounded like two wild
cats."

"Sorry." I was probably blushing, but also felt that
boyish pride of having scored and done it well.

"Oh don't be." His chuckle was deep and
controlled. "Married?"

"I...not now." I looked at the petunias that Sandy
had planted in the pots on the deck and could almost see
her kneeling beside them, smiling and nestling the soil
around them. I hoped that Mark could not see the tears
forming in my eyes.

"That's the best way." He raised his glass toward
the sky. "Peach-moon." Cigar smoke swirled around his
angular face.

"It's beautiful." I stepped to the railing. The cat
hunted in the night from under a chair.

"No, man. Means trouble's coming." He flicked an
ash off his cigar.

I checked to make sure the cat hadn't jumped off
the deck and finished the rest of my brandy. "What do
you mean?"

He waved his cigar. "Means things are going to
change."

I stared down at the dark wood, then up at a fuzzy peach-moon. "I think they already have. More brandy?"

"I'm good, bad, except for the brandy. Thanks, James. Goodnight." He flicked an ash off his cigar onto the freshly cut grass below, and his sliding door creaked when he closed it behind him.

"Goodnight." The clouds swirled around the peach-moon, and I poured another glass. The brandy whirled around my glass while I stood in the dim light. Puffs of clouds appeared from the dark sky occasionally diffusing the moon's light. It did look like a fuzzy peach with a face.

I brought the cat inside. He loved it out there in the dark. Robin and Cynthia were curled-up on the couch. I carried Cynthia up to the bedroom first. She didn't wake except for a tiny mumble. I laid her on the bed and snuggled the comforter around her body that looked so tiny in the large bed. Downstairs, I sat next to Robin. She awoke, startled and crossed her hands over her face. "Where's Cynthia?" she asked.

"Upstairs."

She uncovered her mascara-stained cheeks. "Is she okay?"

"She's fine, sleeping." I offered her a brandy which she accepted. I topped off my glass and then rubbed her back. "She's fine."

"I'm sorry, James. I didn't want to get you involved in this, but I had nowhere else…" Her shaking hands lifted the brandy to her lips. Her throat convulsed. I refilled her glass.

"It's all right." I ran my fingernails up and down her back.

"No it's not all right." She stood, spilling some brandy on her jeans, and walked out onto the deck. I followed. The peach-moon still hovered over the townhouses as if it were a witness to something that I had

not yet seen, but had somehow experienced. I attempted a
smile. Robin paced the deck.

"There's more brandy," I said.

"She...I can't believe that bastard did that."

"I'm right here."

She turned and after a slight stumble on the deck
boards, she wrapped her arms around me, squeezing me
against her. I stroked her soft hair while her tears
moistened my shirt, and the peach-moon swam toward
the other side of the sky.

"Cynthia seemed fine when I put her into ou...my
bed." She looked up. Twisted knots of ropes filled my
gut. "I'll sleep on the couch tonight."

"James, I'm sorry about--"

"It'll be fine."

We watched the moon journey toward the west,
unfettered by the few strands of clouds that slipped by in
its peachy light.

"She's adorable."

Robin rubbed her hand against my chest. She
looked away. "Cynthia is my niece."

"She likes chocolate like you."

She turned and smiled.

"See how the moon is smiling back at you?"

"James, I don't know--"

"Look, I'll sleep on the couch tonight, doc. We
can talk about this when you're ready."

She nodded. We walked up the stairs. The cat
followed, swatting at our heels. Cynthia's tiny hand
gripped one of the pillows. Robin caressed her hair and
whispered something. She looked at me as if I were some
form of saint and rubbed her hand on my shoulder. "I'll
feel safer if you're here with us." She pulled me into the
bed. It was an unusually warm feeling. Normally if I were
next to Robin in bed, my thoughts would be consumed
with the anticipation of feeling her body and her passion.

However, this new, almost confusing feeling, was far more powerful. I was there to protect and comfort. I rubbed Robin's back while she gently stroked Cynthia's arm until I could hear their breaths elongate and deepen.

The cat sits on my chest. "My name is Oliver," he says.

"I know."
"Well quit calling me 'the cat.'"
"Sorry."
"And you should be." He licks his right paw.

Oliver was sitting at the door waiting for me to wake. He curled his back, twitched his tail and rubbed his whiskers against the doorframe. Cynthia curled up in a ball and stared blankly away from me. They were both hungry, as was I. I looked for Robin, updated Oliver's food and tried to figure out what Cynthia needed. Fortunately, Robin had left a note on the coffee table:

> Hi James,
> I'm very sorry about last night. Thank you so much for being so kind and understanding. I really appreciate it.
> Cynthia's a good girl. I couldn't take her with me. I'm leaving her in your care. I'll be in touch soon.
> She likes FruitLoops for breakfast, fried chicken, and cucumber and mayonnaise sandwiches on white toast.
> Robin
> Please take care of both of you. You two are all I have.

The last two sentences frightened me. I wondered what they really meant and wondered where Cynthia's parents were. I worried about Robin and about my ability to look after such a young girl.

I was becoming much more familiar with the grocery store again--Cynthia too. When we strolled up

the cereal section, she ran to the FruitLoops and
exclaimed, "Can we have these? It's got a prize."
          I knelt beside her. "Okay, but can you do me a
small favor?"
          "Uh huh."
          "Say, it has a prize.'"
          She looked at me for a moment. "It has a prize."
          "Put it in the cart."
          Our smiles wilted in the checkout line. The twig
of a woman behind us looked at Cynthia, and then
scowled at me. I looked at Cynthia and realized how dirty
her face, legs and rumpled clothes were. Meanwhile,
Cynthia attempted to sneak a role of candy onto the
conveyer.
          "Do you have a Shop-Right Card?" The cashier
looked at me through weary and impatient hazel eyes.
          "No…my wife…" A vision of Sandy strolling
through the store with another man flashed in my mind
like a bright light that shuts one's eyes.
          "What's the phone number?"

          I didn't know that I was shopping incorrectly. I ate
some FruitLoops too, but Cynthia ate the cereal with a
precise system--one color at a time. She fished for the
prize in the box quite unsuccessfully. We poured the
contents into a large bowl and found the toy. She danced
the little purple animal across the coffee table while I
tried to figure out what to do with a five-year-old girl.
She was too small for a shower. So I suggested a bath.
She definitely needed one. She seemed nervous about the
whole thing--probably not as much as I was. I filled the
hot tub relatively shallow, just above the jets. I wasn't
sure what to do next, how to bathe a little girl. The water
temperature seemed right. I showed her the tub. Her hand
gripped behind my knee.

She looked up at me. "I don't have to touch Mister Walrus do I?" Her eyes stared at me as if I possessed the answer to some eternal question.

"No." My face felt sunburned and sweaty since that term seemed to imply only one thing. "Do you need help getting in the tub?"

"Yes." She had trouble wriggling out of her dress and panties. Then I picked her up and eased her into the tub. "Will you wash my hair too? Daddy always..." She stopped splashing.

"Okay." I fumbled around until I found the most gentle shampoo in the bathroom, some soap and a washcloth.

"Is Oliver gonna be nice to me."

"He better." I held the back of her head and nervously placed my other hand on her belly while we dipped her hair back into the water. "There." I lathered up the shampoo and tried not to let any drip into her eyes. "Where is your Daddy?"

"He left me with Grand Daddy."

"Your mother?"

"Mommy's sick."

"Okay. Ready?" She leaned back to rinse again with my left hand on the back of her head and my right washing out the lather. She slid in the tub, her head almost submerging, and I quickly grabbed her to pull her up. I removed my right hand from her tiny butt and thigh and looked away embarrassed. She seemed startled at first, but we managed to remove the suds from her hair.

I handed her a bar of soap. "Okay, I did the hair, can you do the rest?"

"Okay."

I left her there splashing in the tub. "Call me when you're done."

I sat in the living room and wondered about Daddy and Mister Walrus. I looked around the room and realized how unsafe it was for a child--sharp table edges, electrical cables for the stereo, stairs, small knives and medicine within reach. In a panic, I moved all of the cleaning solutions from under the kitchen sink to a top shelf in the cabinets and searched for anything else that might be harmful.

My home which was earlier a haven had become a threat. I felt as though I were inside a closet filled with dangerous objects…including me. Even the thought that I might be aroused by seeing this naked little girl became confusing. Then I wondered what would happen to Cynthia if Stone came to arrest me. I hadn't discussed the investigation of Sandy's death with Robin. I had simply told her that it was unsolved. I had not told her that I was a suspect. I had lied to her to spare her any worry, but as I sat waiting for Cynthia to finish her bath, I realized that I had lied in order not to lose her.

The Walrus

Cynthia's screams overcame the sudden rumbling of the hot tub jets and my worries regarding Robin. I don't remember the stairs, just Cynthia's tears after I turned the jets off. I raised her from the tub and wrapped her in a green towel. She was trembling, her legs kicking. As I dried her off, she kept sobbing, "no." It took some time to calm her, but we eventually entered the closet to pick out a tee shirt for her. I showed them to her.

"I like this one with shiny stuff." She chose one from Dallas which ironically boasted the name of a strip club. She then advised me that her hair needed to be brushed. We sat on the bed, and I brushed her soft hair in a seemingly unsatisfactory fashion. She expressed my incompetence while my hands shook, and my gut twisted as I thought about her fear of Mister Walrus. The only pain that exceeded what I felt thinking about the bastard who would do such a thing to such a sweet girl was the pain I had felt the afternoon I was told of Sandy's murder.

Downstairs, I placed Cynthia on the couch, looked at the books surrounding us wondering what help they might offer, what wisdom, and realized that I possessed nothing suitable for a little girl to read. Faulkner's *Sanctuary* certainly seemed inappropriate. We agreed on a television station, and after I loaded her clothes into the washer, I wandered out onto the deck to clear my head. The August sun beat down upon me. Sweat oozed into my eyes. I had spent months trying to understand the mind of a rapist. I could find the dots and connect them in terms of raping a woman or a teenage girl who was probably already sexually active. The first dot appeared to be insecurity or some form of repressed trauma. Next came the need to control. Sexual drive seemed an obvious catalyst. Murder appeared to be either a cathartic revenge or simply a way to escape the crime. I regret that I had discovered a place within me that understood these desires. In the case of molesting a five-year-old girl, I could not connect the dots or even find them. It was incomprehensible to me, and I wanted it to remain a mystery. That seemed an abyss from which I would never return. Then a most disturbing thought occurred to me. Cynthia's candor, the matter of fact way she asked me whether or not the bath included Mister Walrus, forced me to consider the fact that she might be damaged for life. Killing Mister Walrus had dots and connections that rather appealed to me.

I pulled the splinters from the deck rail out of my palms. I wiped the sweat from my eyes and went inside. I couldn't hear the washer and went downstairs to find her clothes already done. I transferred Cynthia's clothes from the washer to the dryer and acquired my writing notebook from my office. When I arrived back upstairs, Cynthia was frowning. "Why won't Oliver play with me?"

"He just doesn't know you yet, honey."

"Where's Aunty Robin?"

"I'll call her in a minute."

She crossed her arms across her chest.

I went to Oliver's toy basket and grabbed his favorite--one I had made for him out of string and wrapping ribbons. He had always ignored the ones that Sandy and I had bought for him, but he would have been near death to resist the one I had made for him for less than a quarter. I whipped the string out, and the ribbons dangled like a fishing lure. Oliver crouched. His orange face wiggled as I drew the ribbons across the floor. On the second toss, he pounced. Cynthia giggled. I handed her the string. She freed it from his grasp and tossed it out toward him. This continued for quite some time while I sat in my chair trying to figure out what errand Robin was performing.

"Cynthia, honey, you need to let him catch it sometimes."

"Okay."

After awhile, they both became weary of the sport, and Cynthia returned to the candy and cartoons. The phone's ring interrupted my confused thoughts.

"This is James." There was the recognizable pause of a telemarketing call.

"Mr. James Douglas please."

"Yes, how can I help you?"

"Do you own a house?"

"What do you want."

"Well do you own your own home?" The doorbell rang.

"How the hell can I help you?"

"I guess you can't with that attitude." Click.

I opened the door. There stood Detective Stone with a cigarette drooping from his frowning lips. "May I come in? We need to talk," he said. I widened the door and waved him in. He limped up the steps as usual. "Who's this?" He pointed at Cynthia.

"A friend's niece, Cynthia."

He bent over her and reached out his thick hand. "I'm Detective Stone."

She placed her hand in his. "Hi."

"It's a pleasure to meet you, Cynthia. I need to speak with Mr. Douglas in private for a minute."

"We can step out on the deck. Will you be okay here, Cynthia?"

"Uh huh."

Stone declined my offer for a soda, and we stepped onto the deck.

"News regarding the case?" I asked.

He turned and looked out into the development. "Nice deck." He lit his cigarette.

"Thanks." I rolled up my shirt sleeves.

"This is a bit awkward."

I walked to the other side of the deck, the boards creaking under my bare feet.

He turned toward me and exhaled gray smoke that disappeared into the warm summer breeze. "We had to release Mr. Brown today."

I grabbed the railing.

"We can't place him at the scene of the crime."

"That's it, over?"

"Not exactly." He leaned toward me. "Did you know about the affair?"

"No. I mean she came home late a lot, but she worked long hours."

He stepped toward me. "How were you two getting along?"

"We already went through this, the usual squabbles."

"Like?"

"Just the typical things. I want to read, and she wants to go to some restaurant where you wait two hours for a table to be served food that I could have cooked better--that kind of stuff."

"You didn't suspect anything?"

"If I didn't trust her, I wouldn't have married her."

He looked away. "You know you're lucky, Mr. Douglas."

I walked back toward him. "Having my wife murdered and being questioned like a suspect?"

"No. My wife did the same thing you did. She ate a bottle of pills and drank a bottle of gin dry." He looked down at his scuffed, black shoes. "It caused a stroke, and now she can hardly speak. I'm one of the few people who can understand her." He looked up. "Like I said, you're lucky."

"I guess…thank you for taking me to the hospital."

"You called me Detective Phone that night."
I knelt down and checked the moisture in the
flower pot's soil. "Sure I can't offer you a soda or some
coffee?"

"I need to examine your wife's things again."

"They're still here. I want to get them to her
family soon. I'm sure you understand."

We walked back in, and Cynthia was giggling at
the TV. Stone limped up the stairs ahead of me. "Were
you two having sex?"

"Pardon?"

He turned around on the landing. "How was your
sex life?"

"It appears mine was crappy, and Sandy's was
good." We reached the top of the stairs. "All her things
are in these two rooms and the bathroom here." I gazed at
the brown whicker stand over the toilet--the stand that I
had assembled for Sandy as a surprise for Christmas. "We
had separate bathrooms." I looked down at my neglected
toenails. "Thought that would be good for a marriage."

"I won't be long." He limped into what used to be
Sandy's office. I descended the stairs. Cynthia seemed
fine. I went down to the basement and collected her
clothes from the dryer. Upstairs, I waited for the cartoon
to end.

"I like Bugs Bunny."

"You've never seen him before?" I asked. Her hair
looked just like Robin's, brown and wavy, and her eyes
seemed a smaller version of Robin's.

"How come Oliver won't let me pet him?" She
bounced her bare heels against the couch.

"He will. I washed your clothes."

Stone limped down the stairs. He made some
notes on his pad. "We're done with the rest of your wife's
things, except for the few things that we have at the
station."

I nodded.

Cynthia scooted off the couch and walked over to Stone. "You're a policeman?"

"Yes." He seemed more vibrant than any other time I had seen him. His coal-colored eyes glowed. He pulled out his badge and handed it to Cynthia. He looked at me. "You know, a jealous husband makes for a good suspect."

I had no idea how to respond. Cynthia saved me by asking Stone if he had a gun and caught bad guys like on the cartoons. He knelt in an awkward fashion, his leg clearly bothering him. Cynthia handed back the badge. "Yes, I catch bad guys, so you be good to your mom and dad now."

Cynthia frowned and looked away.

Stone rose and limped to the door. "I'll be in touch." He looked at Cynthia who was now fiddling with the candy. "Nice meeting you, Cynthia."

"Thank you for letting me hold your badge." Her resilience amazed me. One minute she was clearly feeling upset, and the next she was caring and polite. After Stone left, it occurred to me that she must be hungry, particularly since I was. She confirmed my suspicion.

We walked into the kitchen. "Chef James at your service, madam. What would you like to eat." I used a poor French accent, but she laughed.

"Cucumbers."

"Oh, but that is not what Chef James can cook the best." I sliced up a cucumber, picked her up, set her on the counter island, and she picked at them. "Now, I will show you a secret recipe. You must be very quiet. Tell no one."

She wiped her hand on the tee shirt. "Is it good?"

I knelt before her. "It is fit for a princess. But it is a secret for only a princess like you," I rose waving the cooking spoon, "and Chef James. First, we must open the tuna." I bit the can. "It does not open." Cynthia recommended a can opener of course. These antics continued while I prepared a couple of tuna melts. I showed her all the ingredients, and swore her to secrecy. Her laughter dispelled all other thoughts, and for just a brief time, there was nothing but the two of us enjoying the most fundamental elements of living--food and companionship. At first she was a bit awkward about the tuna melt, but then ate it very quickly. After I cleared the table, she applauded Chef James who bowed very humbly to the princess. We then decided to draw pictures for awhile. I tried to draw a bird and she a cat. Her drawing was far better than mine, and it soon became clear that she might need a nap. So too did Chef James.

We went upstairs and lay down. My thoughts became restless. Cynthia cuddled up to me and in a sleepy voice said, "You're funny." I waited until she began a light snore and went downstairs to my office and checked my voicemail which was empty. I saved and closed the file for my novel. I simply couldn't contemplate rape and murder and began to organize the manuscripts in my office. There were so many copies of various works, research notes, bills and the ridiculous piles of paper involving the house--the warranty, the insurance, health insurance, car insurance, insurance for insurance. I organized my research notes and manuscripts, placed all the noise of the endless paper of contemporary living into one pile and became confused as to how to file the limited court records regarding the murder of my father and brother. It was the first time I had returned to the notes about Francis the Ax Man since reviewing them on the Metro before I was dumped off at Woodley Park. I took the notes up to the living room and thought about Francis the Ax Man. I wondered why he had killed my father and brother. When he was alive, the kids were afraid of him, but we sort of picked on him too.

He was an old, weird, black man in ragged clothes who walked around the college mumbling and using an ax as a walking stick.

Later, a thirsty and bleary-eyed Cynthia wandered down the stairs into the living room and sat on the couch. I gave her a glass of juice. Oliver, refreshed from his nap, jumped up on the back of the couch in a playful manner and hunched his back. Cynthia became wide awake. I handed her the string. "He wants to play." I heard keys jingling at the door. Robin walked up the stairs. She was still dressed in jeans and a polo shirt. Cynthia dropped the string and ran to greet her. I stood. Oliver ran upstairs.

"Are you okay, sweety." Robin's eye still looked painful.

"We did lot's of stuff. I played with Oliver." Robin hugged her and then set her on the couch. "And Chef James made a secret recipe." She scooted off the couch, ran into the dining room and then returned with the pictures that we had drawn. "And I drew a picture for you." She handed it to Robin. "It's Oliver."

"That's pretty. This is for me?"

"Uh huh. And Chef James washed my hair."

"Not too well I'm afraid." I sat down. I could tell that despite the glimpse of joy in Robin's expression, she had something serious on her mind.

"James, we need to talk."

I didn't like the sound of that. "Cynthia, would you draw a picture for Chef James too?"

"Okay."

I led Cynthia to the dining-room table, placed her on the chair and handed her the pencil and pad. "Can you do one of Oliver like when he scared you a little while ago?" She nodded. I returned to the living room.

Robin sat and began twirling her hair. I sat next to her. She grabbed my hand. "James, thank you for taking care of her. It sounds like you two had quite a day."

"We had fun. She's delightful, reminds me of you."

Robin looked away. "It's the divorce. I can't see you for awhile."

"How can I help?"

She turned her head back and looked at me. "I can't talk about this right now."

I cupped her cheek in my hand and turned her lips to mine. After a soft kiss, I told her that there was nothing that I wouldn't do for her. I said that I understood, but I really didn't. She had clearly decided her course, and I figured the best thing I could do was simply be both flexible and supportive. Then Oliver came down the stairs and requested his evening meal. I went to the kitchen and invited Cynthia to help. I put the moist food into the bowl and handed it to her.

"Now, put this on his food mat, and if you are very slow, he might let you pet him."

It worked. Cynthia looked up while stroking his back. "He's so soft." Robin smiled at me. After Cynthia changed back into her now clean clothes, Robin told Cynthia it was time to go. I reminded Robin to take the pictures that Cynthia had drawn for her. After Cynthia protested about how she wanted to play with Oliver, I told her that Oliver would come visit her in her dreams. The house felt so empty. The peaceful silence that I craved when I wrote was almost unbearable. Cynthia had stirred up foggy memories of my own childhood, little snapshots. I struggled for awhile to focus these splinters of thought into something coherent. I tried to remember something good about my childhood, but I eventually became exhausted and went to bed.

"Christ, you're stoned again."

"Yeah that's me, Mom."

She's pointing the knife at me. "I'm not going to have drugs in this house."

71

*"What's for dinner?" My stomach growls,
munchies. I want some munchies.*

*"Where's your bother? Go get him and get
cleaned up for supper."*

*The potato chips look good. The bag is in my
hand. Salty chips, yes.*

*A sharp pain on my cheek. "I'll slap you again,"
Mother says.*

*The chips are gone. "Who are you to talk? Out all
night. Think I don't hear the fighting?"*

*She slaps again. I catch her forearm in time.
"Don't ever hit me again, bitch."*

"Get out. Get out."

I don't like the knife in her hand.

*I'm in a field now, and Susan is dancing around
me chanting, "You got in trouble. You got in trouble."
The field is spinning. "You're my playmate. We're
connected forever."*

My chest and forehead dribbled beads of sweat as
I sprang up from under the comforter. After I caught my
breath, I found only darkness except for the clock which
read 3:23 a.m. I walked downstairs, breathing through my
mouth and clogged nose. A brandy soothed my dry
throat, and cable offered a black and white John Wayne
film. Wayne plays a dark character who wears a white
hat. I drifted off to sleep before the ending.

Oliver's cries for his food woke me around ten.
Some self-help talk show blared into the room. I
wondered why self help required a show. The dry food
clattered into his dish. I called Robin who was
unavailable. After a shower and some canned fruit, I tried
to work on the novel. I sat for hours and typed only one
sentence--a poor one. All I could think about was Robin,
about cooking for her and Cynthia. After I ate some more
canned fruit, the doorbell rang. I rushed to the door
hoping to find Robin standing on the landing, but two

young men stood there in blue blazers holding *Bibles*.
"How can I help you?"
"May we come in and share the word of God?"
"Which one?"
"Christ, our savior."
"Which word?"
He held the *Bible* up. "Have you read the *Bible*?"
"Yes. I have it in my fiction section. As I file
books by author, I'm not sure where to place it
sometimes. Currently, it's filed under PPP."
"PPP?"
"P-cubed. Post-Post-Post modern fiction."
"We're here to collect donations for--"
"Hey, ask God." I closed the door. "God is
omniscient, omnipotent--just can't handle money. It
seems he's always broke. If God is a he."

The dreams came despite the booze. I couldn't
stop them. If it wasn't the terrified face of Susan Toller or
the decomposed face of Sandy, it was Robin's avoidance
and Cynthia's sobs. I tried to reach Robin on the phone
without success and developed a devoted relationship
with bourbon and aspirin.
I performed those duties that Sandy usually
addressed--changed the litter, vacuumed, ran the
dishwasher. I missed Sandy's laugh really. I missed her
peeking out the of blinds, her love for popcorn that she
chewed with her mouth open, how lovely she looked in
her blue evening gown and the way she smiled as we left
for an event. There was a sweetness about her that
complimented her resolve. I had never been in love
before I met Sandy. Sleep remained an abject function
bereft of solace.
I wasn't sure how many days had passed. They all
seemed functionary and endless. I started skipping class. I
didn't even have the structure of going to class to remind

me that time was slowly moving forward. Nor did I have
a reason not to pour a drink early in the afternoon. It was
a Thursday, I think. I turned off the air conditioning and
opened up the house. The evening, August breeze cleared
some of the gloom while the orange sun slowly hid
behind the fluttering, green leaves of the tall oaks.

Oliver's food plinked into his bowl. I closed the
bag, stared at the bottle of bourbon but knew I should
probably eat instead. I called the local Chinese place. In
addition to the special double-cooked pork, szechuan
style with peppers and onions, I ordered some fried rice
and soup to meet the delivery minimum. It always made
me chuckle when I spoke to the order taker, a woman
with a thick Chinese accent named Tracy. I flipped on the
cable, food-fight news until I couldn't stand five people
yelling at once regarding a Senator's affair with an intern
and cruised through the channels until the cartoons
seemed best. The doorbell rang. I collected the cash on
the table and opened the door. There stood a tall man in a
light-gray suit.

"I don't need any more *Bibles*." I started to close
the door.

"I'm Kevin Brown. May we talk?"

Maybe it was the melodic nature of his voice, or
perhaps it was my fatigue, but I resisted the temptation to
throw him off the landing. I probably shouldn't have, but
I let him in. We stood in the living room sizing each other
up.

"I have bourbon and coke." I said.

"Bourbon, neat."

I waved toward the love seat and returned with
two full glasses. I handed one to him. He drank half of it
down in one gulp. He looked at the bookcases. "I
understand you're trying to be a writer."

"Trying is the operative part of the phrase."

He leaned forward placing his elbows on his knees and then rolling the glass between his palms. "I know this is awkward. I didn't kill her."

I searched for a response.

"James right? I'll find the SOB who did. She did love you--"

"And fucking you." I stood thumping my glass on the coffee table.

He emptied his glass. His blond hair was perfectly neat, like his drink. He loosened his yellow tie. I went to the kitchen and returned with the bottle and handed it to him. He replenished his glass. I wondered what good it would do to be jealous of someone regarding someone who was dead.

He looked up. "It's ruining my marriage."

"Mine is sure in great shape."

"I'm sorry. I didn't kill her."

"What is it you want?" I sipped the bourbon.

"To find the killer."

The doorbell rang. Tracy's sister, Jan, which she pronounced Jenz, received a generous tip, and I received her delightful smile and a hot bag of food. I paused in the foyer wondering what to do and invited Kevin to dinner. Maybe it was my curiosity. We sat in the dining room, he where Sandy used to sit.

"This is good," he said.

"They make it special for me."

He smiled.

As I ate, the fog of the booze started to lift, and I started to understand why Sandy was attracted to Kevin. He possessed a kind yet not obsequious demeanor that fostered acceptance, a confidence and yet a slight insecurity that comes from experience. Despite the fact he had been sleeping with my wife, I kind of liked him. It felt quite strange.

"We were high school sweethearts," he said while I picked up the plates. "One day she told me she was pregnant, and I insisted on an abortion. We never spoke again until I moved to D.C. and ran into her at her law firm." I put the dishes in the sink and walked back to the table.

"You were fucking MY WIFE." I grabbed the back of his suit, raised him from the chair, spun him around, and with my left hand holding his lapel, raised my right in a fist and delivered a hard right cross to his face. He fell against the pine bookshelves which subsequently fell on top of him along with the books and crystal. The crash seeped slowly into my ears as I stepped toward him, my fingernails kneading my palms. A piece of crystal crunched under my step. I paused, staggered and grabbed a chair which toppled along with me to the floor.

I slowly gathered the pieces of crystal into my hands and heard Kevin righting the bookshelf. "Her mother's crystal," I said.

When I stood with the slivers of glass in hand, Kevin was replacing the books upon the shelves. After tossing the pieces of crystal into the trash, I knelt and gathered some of the novels. I looked at Kevin and handed them to him. "Look at your blazer." I pointed. He looked down. I went to the kitchen and returned with a moist towel and pointed at the blood oozing from his nose. "I'll take care of the books later. The booze is next to the couch." He sat, and I handed him a drink.

"Next time I'm going to block," he said. He dabbed his nose.

"That would probably be a good idea." I sat nearby. "Look I'm--"

"Don't apologize. I'd do the same thing I suppose."

"Another drink?"

"Sure." He delivered it with the same Jersey accent as Sandy. We drank for awhile. "Thank you for dinner."

"No sweat."

"And the drinks…I'm sorry."

"Yes."

"I just thought we could find the killer together."

"I'll have to think about that. At present I want to not only show you the location of your spleen, but also its color and taste."

"I understand."

I leaned forward. "And if I was fucking YOUR wife?"

He looked down. "I should go."

He set his half-empty glass on the table and walked toward the door. "Thank you for the dinner and the drinks. I'm sorry."

After he left, I sat down and tried to understand his motivation for contacting me. There appeared to be too many possibilities. He may have thought that I was the killer, or he may have killed her and wanted to find out what I knew. Then again, he may have simply wanted to meet me due to a common bond with Sandy. I finished the bourbon, turned both locks on the door and went to my empty bed.

They Only Come Out at Night

Fur tickles my nose. I reach for warmth. Purring rumbles against my side. The Lion's paws knead my chest. Each time he strokes, the clock ticks another minute, faster and faster. His purring sharpens, quicker now. I smell perfume, fruity. Susan's face floats away into a gray fog. The Lion's tail taps against the bed. I rise upon no feet and cover the Lion with the comforter, his tail tapping more quickly, the clock racing forward, a blur of red digits.

"Susan?"

She moves out the door and down the hall. "I need some makeup now." *She disappears through the door of Sandy's bathroom. I can't find my hands.*

She's applying lipstick, red, now black, and trying to cover her breasts with her torn, soggy sweater. The projector rattles, and the film taps. Lines ripple across the screen.

"Nice eyeliner." *She turns to show me.*

"Please, dark spirit. Please leave me be?"

"You need some makeup too. Cleanse first though."

"How?"

She turns to the mirror. I watch her reflection while she lightly brushes her lashes, and I see that I'm simply a floating head upon an egg-shaped sphere. My face melts into the yellow haze. The fog is cold.

His purring comforts me now.

"Have you been eating my Life Savers?"

He grins and presses his belly against me. "You're cold and look like a luminous egg."

"Sorry."

"That's what you are. Rest now. I'll warm you."

I rose from the bathroom floor. The smell of mold filled my nostrils, and the bourbon swished about my head as I staggered down the stairs to search for bottled water in the refrigerator. It soothed my parched lips but not my anguish. I called Robin for help. She did not respond to my call. Later, I scheduled an appointment with Dr. Fowler and gave her authorization to review Robin's notes regarding my previous treatment.

I drove over to meet Dr. Fowler the following day. I handed Betty, the receptionist, a small bouquet of flowers to thank her for driving me home. She smiled and waved me to sit. A little, redheaded boy sat nearby looking at the mauve carpet. His hands writhed about in his lap as if he were making bread. A tall, blond woman entered the waiting room. "James Douglas?"

"Yes." I stood.

"I'm Dr. Fowler." She extended her hand which I gladly embraced, and we walked back to her office on the opposite side of the floor from Robin's. Fowler's office was meticulously organized. There were no lose pens or paper clips. Her neatly shelved books added color to the white walls and the tan leather furniture. I had to choose between the chair and the sofa. I chose the chair. She sat in hers opposite me, crossed her legs clad in a blue pantsuit and calmly plucked a pen from the black holder. She placed her yellow pad on her knee. I recalled how all the psychology majors in college were so attractive. We exchanged the typical verbal pleasantries. She did what I would have done at a sales meeting. She asked me about safe topics, about my school work, about my writing. Then, she asked me to relax. I knew this meant that the conversation would become serious.

She made a few notes on her pad. "I understand that you recently lost your wife. I'm very sorry."

"It's not your fault." I rubbed the arms of the chair.

She leaned forward. "How long were you and your wife together?"

"We dated for five years. We've been married for almost six…" I looked at the tan sofa.

"Mr. Douglas, I'm here to help. Have you been sleeping?"

"Nightmares mostly." I crossed my legs.

"About?"

"Angels, maybe devils."

"Is Sandy in your dreams?"

"Not yet."

She opened a file and flipped through it. "Dr. Weiner--"

"Robin." My voice rose.

"Robin discussed your entire life with you and documented it in your file during your treatment for cocaine abuse."

"Yes?"

"There is almost an entire year missing?" The clock ticked.

"When?" I pulled a pen from my pocket and started to twirl it around my fingers.

"It seems to be when you were around fifteen."

"Is Robin here today?"

"Why?"

I stood. "I need to see her."

"Please calm down." Her voice was melodic and soothing. I sat. The clock ticked slowly upon her desk as if time and sanity were somehow related. Each tick grew louder and louder. She made a note on her pad. "We were discussing your wife."

"I cannot stop thinking about her. When I'm with her, there is no past. There is no future. There is now."

"Escape?" She crossed her legs.

I stood and started to examine Fowler's books that lined the bookcases next to her desk. "To where might I escape absent a women's love? What life might I conjure absent her caress, her gentle words, her guidance?" I picked up the *Collected Works of Carl Jung.* No dust sifted into the air as I flipped through the pages.

Fowler neatly oriented her yellow pad upon the desk, and her green eyes peered into mine. "Do you miss your wife?"

"Yes. I told you that."

She bent over and picked up my pen that I thought was still in my hand. We exchanged the book and pen. She carefully filed Jung back into his place, and I sat upon the sofa. It crinkled under my weight.

I watched her pick up her pad. "Her notes also mention a brother, Steve?"

"I don't remember..." I looked at the clock.

"You do not remember telling her about Steve, or you do not remember Steve?"

"Yes."

"Why are you rubbing your knees now?"

I looked at her books and remembered how all of my books, being surrounded by them, made me feel safe, like I had felt with father's dusty books.

"Mr. Douglas?"

"I need to know I have my hands. I...the boxes are in the way. I think he has blond hair. It's black, no white now. Yes, it seems blond."

"Whose hair?"

"I'm cooking chicken marsala for her. She'll be home soon."

"Relax, Mr. Douglas."

"She likes it. Well, she says she likes it because of the mushrooms. Got to time it right for her. Never know when she gets home these days. Got's to ask. Damn mules, can't nobody get this mule away from me?"

"What mule, Mr. Douglas?"

"That bitch, always running back to the barn."

"James?"

"Threw me once there in the pasture where..."

Sweat dripped into my eyes. Dr. Fowler was quickly writing some notes. "Mr. Douglas, do you remember what just happened?"

"Call me James. Thank you for handing me my pen."

The clock ticked. "We need to pursue this further. I can work you in," she picked up her black appointment book, "maybe tomorrow?"

"I have a paper due, and Detective Stone wants to meet again."

She stood. "This is important."

"Same time next week?"

She nodded. "Try to get some rest."

The following afternoon, I left Stone a voicemail and sat on the deck reviewing the most recent chapter of my novel. My new neighbor, Mark, slid open his door.

"Hey, man."

"Hi," I said from behind my sunglasses.

He poured some charcoal into his grill. "Having a little party. Come over."

"I need to--"

"Babes are coming by. We're having burgers. Come over in about a half hour." I couldn't tell if his accent came from New York or Alabama. It seemed curiously mixed.

When he opened his door, Mark was wearing white shorts and a red polo shirt that advertised the University of Maryland's Terrapins.

"Hey, man. Come in." He clearly looked like Elvis, and I chose not to mention it for what might be one time too many for him.

"Go Terrapins," I said.

"Go Turtles."

I walked up the steps and handed him the wine and beer that I had quickly procured. "I hope this is okay."

"Help me with the burgers." I did. The burgers spat at the grill as the charcoal fumed the still air hovering the bright pine deck. "They need a flip." I flipped them over. The sizzle spat at me. "Here, the buns." I placed them on the grill briefly.

We sat on the deck eating the sandwiches saying nothing for awhile. Some children ran by beneath yelling in some form of game. Mark pulled some more chips out of the bag. "Heard about your wife. Sorry, man," he said.

"Thank you. This is a great burger."

"You like it?"

I gazed at the children. "She wants to have kids."

"The girls are running late, but they're coming. They'll know how to help." He winked his dark eye.

"What do you do, Mark?"

"Lot's of stuff. Hear you go to college now?"

"Graduate school, writing."

He virtually drenched his second burger in ketchup while the paper plates attempted to escape into a sudden summer breeze before I pressed them down on the pine table.

"Writing what?"

"About cool neighbors who cook great burgers."

He laughed through a mouthful of chips.

After eating and waiting for him to finish his cigar, I insisted on leaving, but Mark persuaded me to stay and have another beer. He convinced me that we needed to toast the Turtles. I declined a cigar. The doorbell rang.

"Here they are," he said, and waved his stocky arms. We went inside. Through the door came two very provocatively dressed young girls--both blond, not necessarily by natural causes.

"James, meet Jamie." I shook her hand, and she smiled as if she knew me. She smelled like tangerines. She sat on the puffy, white leather couch and rubbed her hand for me to sit nearby. Mark and the other girl went upstairs. I sat next to Jamie. The brief conversation felt awkward, and her eyes seemed dreamy and almost completely black as I could not discern the outline of her pupils. Her words came out slowly with a southern charm that sometimes quickened into an almost incoherent pattern. Part of me knew I should leave, but another part definitely wanted to stay.

Mark and the other girl saved me from the conversation by descending the stairs after a few minutes. He slapped her butt as she went into the kitchen.

"You two getting along okay?" He sat in his white leather chair. I nodded. Jamie rubbed my thigh. Mark smiled, and the other girl returned with a bottle of tequila, some sliced lemons and salt. Mark sat up from his recliner. "Show them how we do it, baby." She placed a wedge of lemon between his teeth, licked his tan neck and poured some salt on it. Then she licked the salt, took a shot from the bottle and sucked on the lemon in his mouth--for quite some time. Meanwhile, Jamie picked up a lemon wedge and the salt shaker, and soon her lips were against mine as she sucked on the lemon.

It became my turn, and then it became my turn again. However, I was licking the salt off Jamie's breasts now.

"He wants to watch," she whispered. Soon my head rested on the white leather couch, and Jamie was on top of me. Then, I was on top of her. Then, she was on top of me.

"Yes," I exclaimed. She wiped her lips that offered an impish grin.

"That felt good." She rubbed my chest. "We should do that some more?"

"Bravo. Go Turtles," said Mark.

"I should use the rose lipstick tonight." I follow Susan into the hall. "Maybe peach would look nice?" She turns and giggles. The glare from the vanity lights of Sandy's bathroom dim my sight.

"I like it here?" Susan beckons me to bed. I follow, naked. Jamie sleeps, the blue comforter shrouding her.

The Lion sits above her licking his paw.

Susan points at Jamie. "And will you kill her too, what of Robin...Sandy?"

"Please leave my dreams. Please dark spirit."

She smiles. "Remember, you asked for it."

"Hey, wake up."

I woke on the sand-colored carpet of the hallway that sorely needed a cleaning. Jamie's hazy face came into view when I rolled over.

"What time...?"

"Late," she said. I rose, and Jamie grabbed my morning erection. "Dreaming about me?"

"Who else?"

"Robin," she said with a frost in her voice.

"She...how do you know about--"

"You called me Robin last night during our second round, tiger." She patted my chest.

"I'm sorry."

"Give me a ride home, and I'll forgive you."

"Did I hurt you?"

"Just some sexy spanks while you were behind me, tiger."

"There's some juice, maybe water, in the frig. I'll be down shortly."

After she left the third floor, I splashed some water into my face and smoothed my ruffled hair. I remembered meeting her and the strange sex we had at Mark's house but had no idea how she ended up in my bed for the night. After dressing, I found Jamie sipping some water in the living room.

She wrote her number on the phone pad, and I drove her a few miles to her apartment. She asked me to call later, but I advised her that I needed to attend class that evening despite her tempting smile and figure.

Metro was as wonderful as usual. I walked in a straight line--a concept seemingly foreign to most people. Both men and women crossed my path, but I maintained my course in spite of their stupidity. I wondered which part of walk on the right side of the walk they didn't understand. I bumped into them should they not yield. I had not eaten at all and purchased a hotdog from one of the stands at Dupont Circle. Inside the Brooking's Institute, where class was held, a "Fruit Integration" soda provided a chuckle--affirmative action for fruit.

Given my absence, the instructor asked after me. I advised her that given the environment, I felt much better. My smile was surpassed only by hers. Fortunately this night was one that required no submission from me. I had only darkness and confusion to report. I felt ill, and felt even worse that I was not better prepared. I couldn't focus at all and excused myself at the break to go home.

After the Metro-ride home, I tossed *The New Yorker* in the trash at the Shady Grove stop and walked around the wire-fenced construction toward the parking.

The smell of the soil seeped into every pore. Then the bus fumes overcame any sense of nature.

A woman with yellow hair and a red briefcase touched my arm from behind. I turned in a startle. "The lights are out. Would you walk me to my car?"

"Of course." I smiled. We walked for a few steps along the cement walks that were surrounded by darkened, lantern-like lights hanging upon the fences.

"It's light here now." I pointed. "My car is--"

"Please," she said. She wrapped her thin fingers around my wrist. "I'll give you a lift back to your car."

I walked her down the path. I introduced myself, and I think her name was Rose, a cookbook writer, something about wheat allergies. I declined her offer for a lift despite my complaining bladder, and she drove her light-gray SUV about looking for the exit while I hurried to my car. She drove by me one way, then another. I kept pointing to the exit. She finally arrived there.

Mark knocked on my front door almost immediately following my relief of the pending dampening of my jeans.

"Heard the garage open."

"How is Mark doing?"

"Let's go pick up Jamie."

"I…she's nice and all but--"

"You balled the hell out of her." He slapped me on the back.

"It's late."

"It's early. She's waiting."

We drove through the evening gloom to acquire Jamie, and then we stopped in a dark parking lot to wait for her after she stepped out of the car. While large drops of rain began to patter the roof and windows, Mark moved into the back seat.

After her return, the street lamps sped by as I felt the boyish need to show-off the power of my BMW that needed a wax.

"The blow is $275," she said.

We arrived back at my place. She strutted into the kitchen as if she owned it. I advised Mark to leave with her and the cocaine. However, she had already plucked a plate from the kitchen and poured some powder on it and set it upon the coffee table. Mark smiled.

After they snorted a few lines, Mark ushered me aside. "Hey, man, can you cover this? I'll get you back."

Jamie was kind enough, or perhaps evil enough, to leave a gram or so upon the plate after I handed her three hundred. They left. The only bill left on the money clip was a five. A beer seemed to be the best way to resolve my hangover. The only thing on cable was either some soap opera porn or banter about a Congressman's sex scandal. I turned the volume down and caressed the dusty books next to me, even the post modern ones. I stared at my manuscript and wondered why I wasn't pulling Jamie's hips into mine. The cocaine stared at me, and I somehow managed to merely taste it with my moistened finger to my tongue. I worried what Robin would think.

The rain began slapping against the windows sounding as if my home were inside a car wash. I searched for the tuning fork for my guitar unsuccessfully but tuned it fairly well by ear. I began a love ballad and during the fourth stanza, noticed water dripping upon the black polish of her and then running across the bridge of her strings. The pile of powder stared back at me. I set the brown guitar pick next to the plate. The door bell rang. I stepped into the foyer and unlocked the door. Then, I remembered that there was a pile of cocaine on the table and worried that it might be Stone with another one of his surprise visits.

The door pushed open. "That bitch, Cindy." A drenched Jamie pushed by me. Her short, red skirt rose to reveal the absence of panties as she walked up the steps into the living room and plopped upon the couch. I returned from the kitchen with a towel and a cold beer. I opened the beer for her and proceeded to dry her hair.

She picked up my money clip, stripped the five away from the credit cards and quickly rolled it into a straw. "You've hardly touched this?" She sniffed. The sound of her clogged nostrils seemed painful, but she smiled. "You play guitar?" She pointed to them.

"I play around with her."

She stood and went into the kitchen. I heard the water running at the sink and heard her sniffing. I knew she was sniffing the water to clear her clogged nose like I once did.

Susan stood before me. "Why do you haunt me so?" I asked.

"What?" said Jamie as her soaked, red heels clicked during her return to the room. She sat.

"Do you not see her? There, upon the stairs, stealing away?"

"Have a line." She handed the bill toward me.

"You don't see her?"

"Play a song for me."

"How can..." I stood and followed Susan. The oak banisters felt cold and yet offered some semblance of assurance. I turned. "You did not see her?"

"Here."

I returned to Jamie. "Did you not see her?"

"Who?" She handed me the bill and then wiped the tears from my cheeks.

"There."

Susan was naked now. "She cannot cleanse you."

"Who can?"

"James, who are you talking to?" asked Jamie.

"Damn it. She's gone again. Quiet, maybe she'll come back and tell me."

"Tell you what?"

"I don't know yet."

"Who?"

"It."

"What's wrong?" asked Jamie.

Susan sat next to us on Sandy's couch. Susan smiled, her hair streaked with sleet. I pushed Jamie away and looked at Susan.

"I was trying to help," I said. Susan turned away.

"Who are you talking to?" Jamie said. Her blond eyebrows crinkled toward her tiny nose.

"She sits right here, next to me. Do you not see her?"

"No. I want to feel you inside me now."

"She's sitting right here."

"Mark told me about your wife--"

"No it's..." I turned to Susan. "Why are you here?"

Susan stood before the bookcase. "Nice grammar books you have." She thumbed through them. "Chicago, APA is better really. Don't you think?"

"Necessity I suppose," I said. I stood.

"Hug me, James." The Lion sat next to Jamie.

I reached out, and Susan opened a book on the table. Its pages fluttered. She twirled a pen and then circled Ophelia.

Jamie was pale and sweaty. I could almost see her heart's rapid motion. Jamie stood as I read a few pages of the play.

"Did you?" Jamie walked for the door and turned toward me. "Did you see that?"

"Did you see her?"

"Wind. It was wind or something. I need another drink and a line."

"Don't sit too close to the Lion."

"You're nuts." She laughed, sat and lined some more of the numbing powder. I went to the refrigerator to acquire more beer for us both. She preferred it simply in the can like me. Susan stood flipping the pages.

"It's drafty in here," Jamie said. Her shoulders twitched.

Sanctuary

I'm hiding the coke now. Cops. Shadows watching. I know they're there. My feet struggle to feel the carpet. I walked through the gray fog of the diffused morning light, stumbled into the door jam, then caught my fall on the bathroom sink. The seat of the toilet creaked, and I sat down to avoid aiming or waking. I rinsed my hands afterward and went back to bed. Despite the August heat, the comforter felt warm and reassuring, and I wrapped the pillow over my face to shut out the growing light. I don't know how long I lay there feeling the shuddering within me. It felt like a waterfall running through me. I was not asleep. Nor was I awake. I became more afraid to dream than to wake. I pulled the pillow off my face and sat up, my head throbbing and my mouth dry. The sleepy dirt in the corners of my eyes felt crunchy to my fingers. Then I noticed the blood on my hands. I pulled the comforter away from Jamie. She lay there on her side, her face covered in blood. I turned her onto her back. She stirred slightly. Her neck throbbed with an erratic pulse, and I asked her to wake while rubbing both her shoulders. She groaned. She sat up and grabbed her forehead. While she sat there, I went into the bathroom and prepared a damp washcloth. The cool water felt reassuring on my hands, and I hoped that it would do the same for Jamie's forehead. I looked around the room to see if Susan or the Lion were there watching.

Jamie's eyes were dilated, her speech slurred. I dabbed the blood off her face and soon realized that her nostrils were clogged with blackened, dried blood. She pushed my hands away.

"Where're my clothes, tiger?" She moved to the edge of the bed.

I picked up her red miniskirt and black tee shirt and handed them to her. After we both dressed, I helped her down the stairs. I saw the plate of coke still resting on the coffee table and quickly diverted her into the kitchen for some water. While she was drinking it, I went back into the living room and put the plate into an end table drawer.

She walked in. "Hey, we had fun last night. You were kind of goofy."

I sat down in my chair, and she on the couch.

"Lions and some ghost...Susan. Who's Susan?" She fumbled with her red pumps.

"Nobody. You need to drink some more water."

She pulled the back strap of her shoe over her heel. "I need a couple lines. What happened to the plate?"

"We must have finished it." I closed the drawer of the end table. "You need a break, Jamie."

"Oh, this happens, no big deal." She dabbed her nose with a tissue. "I need to see Sean. Can you give me a ride, tiger?"

"I can take you home."

"Sean'll take care of me." She pulled a brush out of her purse and began stroking it through her fine, yellow hair.

A sense that she might be in trouble yielded to my desire to simply get her out of my house. I drove her to Sean's place, a little apartment in a rather ugly neighborhood. She gave me a peck on the cheek and asked me to call later. I said that I would check on her soon. While driving home, I could only think about getting away.

I was relieved that Susan left me alone while I packed. The house seemed smaller, and when I pulled out another shirt, one of Sandy's pair of pajamas fell off the shelf in my closet. They felt soft and fresh, powder blue. I held them against my face and walked down the hall. I don't know how long I stood at the closed door to her office or how long I stood among her things inside, smelling the fabric softener in her pajamas. Oliver came in and curled around my legs, his tail twitching. I ushered him out, set the pajamas on Sandy's desk and closed the door. I had put off packing her things but knew that I soon had to embrace the fact that Sandy was gone. After I checked the locks and put a couple days of food and water out for Oliver, I threw my bags into the car and left.

I had no idea where to go. The mountains seemed like a good idea at first. Then again, sipping a margarita on the beach appealed to my need to escape. I knew it would only be a temporary reprieve from confronting the past and the fear inside me. I headed for Picketsville and tried to ignore the back seat and the rearview mirror in case Susan and the Lion were following.

I drove along the back roads. The bushy, green leaves of the trees were motionless, and the spun bails of hay sat like giant, brown pinwheels on the rolling fields. I stopped briefly to top off the gas tank and bought a pork barbecue. I missed those. For some reason, I could never find a decent pork barbecue in the D.C. area.

I took the bypass around Picketsville, which I found somewhat comical since it was only a mile and a half long. I checked into a cheap motel next to the Interstate just outside of town. I had never stayed at a Motel 6, but this place struck me as a Motel 3. The wallpaper in the room was reminiscent of the horrible color schemes of the early seventies--orange and olive tones that seemed weary like the elderly fellow who was clearly annoyed to have a customer. Aside from the creaky, metal-framed bed and the flower-print lampshade, the only thing that the room needed was a brown, polyester leisure suit draped across the high-school-surplus chair.

I sat in that chair for awhile trying to figure out what I was doing there. I opened my travel bag on the bed and searched for my research notes, but realized that I had forgotten to bring them. I had also forgotten to bring my journal. All I found was a pen.

I drove into town. There was a new shopping center, but I went to the one where I had worked as a bag boy. The grocery store seemed the same. The apples next to the entrance invited me to buy them, and I soon found the shelves with the notebooks. I picked up two, and on the way to check out, I noticed the toys. I added several coloring books and a jumbo set of crayons to my shopping basket.

The woman behind the register was curiously attractive and yet a bit homely. Her skin was almost raw from the sun, and her hazel eyes quickly looked me over.

"Not from around here?" She simply typed the amount into the register--no scanners, no food buying relationship necessary.

"I grew up here."

"Where 'bouts?" She picked up the coloring books.

"Jefferson."

She smiled. "Well now you must know my Daddy then...Watson?"

I thought for a moment. "Mr. Watson...worked at the bookstore?"

"That's Daddy. Books for your daughter?" She had no ring on her finger.

"No, just a special little girl." I handed her a twenty.

"You best wrap it then. Momma's got a shop next door. Wrap it up nice for ya."

She wouldn't let me bag the goods, and her expression seemed to insist on my seeing Momma. The door chime next door clanged, and I entered an antique shop. There were various pieces of carnival glass, mostly orange and yellow, some with hints of green. Some were vases, some bowls. Others appeared to be candy dishes. A shrill voice from behind the shelf startled me.

"Careful around that glass there." A short woman clad in a black, summer dress appeared from behind the dusty shelves. Her hair was gray with some streaks of black left over from her youth. She approached me. "Glass been here awhile. Make you a good deal." Her eyes examined me as if I were a farm animal.

"Your daughter said you could help me."

"Well, what sort of help you need, sonny." She stared at my face, then stepped to my left and looked more closely at the side. "Hmm."

"I just need some wrapping paper." I showed her the coloring books.

She waved her thick arm that was probably once hardened from farm work. The skin wiggled as if in a breeze. "Over here. We'll fix you up." She led me to the wrapping area. I chose a peach color with some blue highlights and handed her the books and the crayons. She began to wrap them. "So, how you know my girl?"

"We just met."

"That's hard to swallow. She knows every bachelor in the county seems like. Besides you look familiar." She tied off the bow.

"I grew up here."

Here dark eyes widened. "You're Eddy's boy."

"My father's name was Edward."

"Edward Douglas. You look just like him. He told us to just call him Eddy, me and Mr. Watson…remember him?" She handed me the package. "For your little one?"

"A friend's. Does Mr. Watson still work at the college bookstore?"

"Shame what happened to your Daddy. That crazy old fool killing him."

"That's why I'm here. I don't understand what happened."

She rang up the price. "Best to leave all that be now."

She then sold me a piece of carnival glass, and I wished her well. I drove over to the college. Jefferson seemed bigger than I remembered, but the freshly cut lawns and the red brick buildings with white trim seemed comforting. I drove past the athletic fields where I had played football with the other professors' kids. The stillness in the air reminded me of the end of summer, when August waned to the coming school year.

I entered the bookstore, and there stood Mr. Watson. He had seemed old twenty-four years ago. He looked the same, tiny glasses beneath a mostly bald head with a fringe of white hair perched as a crescent around the back and sides of it. He fumbled with a text book and then looked at me over the top rims of his glasses.

"Ice cream sandwiches are in the cooler over there." He pointed.

I wandered around the store for a bit and then pulled an ice cream sandwich from the cooler. At the register, I pulled out my money clip.

"Your money's no good here, boy." He locked the register. "Besides, I was just closing up. More trouble than it's worth really."

I looked down at the ice cream. "I haven't had one of these in years."

"Don't you want some Fritos too?" He grinned exposing his yellow teeth.

He was right. I was always harassed for putting Fritos on my ice cream sandwich. "How did you--"

"Was Steve always bought the Fritos." He ushered me out the door and locked it. "I miss your Daddy, always treated me like anyone else. Didn't look down on me like them other teachers."

"How did you know?" I unwrapped the ice cream as we walked toward the parking lot.

"That's what you always bought, James. You want somethin' else?"

"No...No...this is great."

"Mine are the best." He turned toward me. "Where's your car?" I pointed. "Give me a lift home, and the missus'll fix us up somethin' good for supper."

I handed him the keys and sat on the passenger side. I encouraged him to push it. To my amazement, he did. His white hair fluttered in the swift wind coming through the sun roof, and I had never seen him smile so much when we came around the next corner at well over a hundred. He shifted into fifth and kept the petal down. He down shifted and slowed. "You're just like your Daddy." We pulled up to his farm, a large, white house set on a knoll surrounded by evergreen trees and a couple of gray barns beside rows of corn and some smaller gardens. We unfastened our seatbelts, and I closed the sun roof. He tossed me the keys. "She runs nice." We walked up the dirt path to the house. He told me that the missus would soon be home and that we should have a drink before her arrival. We each downed a healthy shot of whiskey. Afterward, he invited me to help pick some corn for supper. There was something honest about tending to the crops that I had forgotten. I could smell the pines and Virginia's red clay. Mr. Watson told me which ears to pick. I had also forgotten about the sharp edges of the leaves.

"Damn it." I grabbed my arm.

Mr. Watson turned around, almost hidden by the draping, green leaves. He pushed them aside. "That one bit you did it?" He laughed. "'Spect we got enough now anyway. Spent too much time up there in the city. Forget about them leaves did you?"

We returned to the house and sat on the edge of the gray, wooden porch that ran the length of the front of it. The tin roof offered some protection from the sun which was now beginning its journey toward the tops of the pines. I pulled the bottom of my black tee shirt out from its tucked position in my jeans and wiped the sweat off my face. I removed my tennis shoes and sweat socks and kneaded my toes into the long blades of grass that tickled the bottoms of my feet.

While we husked the corn, Mrs. Watson and her daughter drove up in a green pickup. The whole thing was rather funny. Mrs. Watson fussed at him for not telling her about a guest for dinner, and he offered various apologies and explanations. Ultimately, Mrs. Watson decided that I needed a good country meal and showed me a better way to remove the ornery corn silk. Mr. Watson and I finished cleaning up the corn and took it around to the back of the house and into the kitchen.

Mrs. Watson inspected it and thanked me. She turned toward her husband. "Where the tomatoes? Can't have no ham without tomatoes." She returned to snapping the green beans into the steaming pot on the wood-burning stove. Mr. Watson pulled me out the door, grabbed a basket on the back porch and led me back out into the still air. We picked a few tomatoes in silence. They were huge compared to the tiny ones that they sold up in the stores near D.C. where you had to be some form of member to get a decent price. As it turned out, I hadn't even been getting a decent tomato. Mr. Watson and I sat with our tomatoes on the front porch.

"That's how it works." He handed me the bottle that he apparently kept hidden behind the metal-framed porch lounger

"Picking tomatoes?" I took a shot.

"Marriage."

"Forgive me, but being yelled at?" I handed back
the pint.

He waved his small hand. "She's gonna holler at
me for somethin'. Might as well know when." He took
another swig. "See, I knew she wanted tomatoes." He
winked at me.

"I don't follow."

"I knew that's what she wanted and gave her a
reason to fuss at me. You'll learn. See, she just wants to
complain, don't much matter about what, just complain,
blow some steam." He smiled. "So I just give her an easy
target. Then it's done, and we get on with things."

"Think she knows?"

He took another swig. "I 'spect so."

The sun slowly turned into a misty, orange wafer
and slid behind the pines that began to turn from green
into black while Mr. Watson asked me why I lived up in
the city. "Nothin' but Jews, Coons and politicians up
there." He handed me the bottle. "Don't do no good for
nobody 'cept themselves." He stood. "And you and me,
we pay for it. Always got their hands out for somethin'."
The boards creaked beneath his boots as he walked to the
edge of the porch.

The soil on my bare feet felt good. He spoke with
a naked honesty that, while somewhat troubling, felt
refreshing like the timid breeze that dried the sweat from
my forehead. I had no response for him at all. Then I saw
the first firefly that I had seen in years. I felt like a
confused boy who simply wanted to find a jar and go
catch it. I fixed my sight on where it had lit, just beyond
the corn. I realized the awful and yet beautiful clarity of
Mr. Watson's words. His bigotry kept him safe. If certain
people had no souls, killing them was like slaughtering a
pig for supper, or killing an adulterous spouse. The firefly
lit again and then another near the porch.

Mr. Watson turned and reached for the pint.
"Dinner's 'bout ready." He hid it behind the lounger. I
brushed the soil off my feet before returning my shoes
and socks to them. We walked around to the back of the
house and into the kitchen. It smelled warm somehow--
fresh ham and beans, the corn ears gurgling in the boiling
pot on the stove. The pale-yellow walls were sprinkled
with various wrought-iron decorations and hangers with
oven mitts and cooking utensils. The kitchen table, set
with five place settings, was covered with a comely white
cloth that was patterned with bright-red apples. Mr.
Watson picked up a fork and started to stir the cobs of
boiling corn. Mrs. Watson told him to sit down with his
guest. We sat, he at the head of the table and I on the side.

She then stepped to the doorway. "Jenny. Get out
of that bathroom and come to supper." Her tone indicated
that this was more than a suggestion. I glanced at Mr.
Watson who fidgeted just like I felt, a boy waiting to be
fed. I wondered if he just wanted to go catch some
fireflies after dinner.

Jenny hurried into the room. "Can I help you,
Momma?"

Mrs. Watson turned from the stove. "Take these
biscuits over to the table." Jenny sat down on the opposite
side of the table from me and placed the biscuits in the
center of the table. Mr. Watson reached for a biscuit.
Jenny tapped his hand. They smiled at each other. Jenny
primped her long, red hair. She had changed into a lovely,
low-cut dress, light in fabric. The white cotton was
decorated with orange flowers and light-green stems that
somehow wrapped around the curves of her body and
then tickled the frills on the neck and shoulder sleeves of
the gown. Her eyelashes were bigger, and her lips far
more full.

"Mathis comin' by tonight?" Mr. Watson asked.

"'Sposed to be here by now," Jenny said.

Mr. Watson looked at me. "Likes my wife's cookin'."

"You hush," said Mrs. Watson when she placed a bowl of steaming ears of corn on the table.

"Momma let me help," Jenny said as if she knew what answer to expect. She was instructed to entertain their guest. "So, Mr.--"

"James. Please call me James."

"What brings you to town?" She fiddled with her silverware.

I looked down at the white plate in front of me and then at Jenny's breasts that appeared to be ripe pears struggling to peek through her dress. "I just needed a break. I'm doing some research." Mrs. Watson placed the beans and ham on the table and sat down.

Mr. Watson chuckled. "'Bout Francis the Ax Man." He stood and walked over to the counter. He returned with the sliced tomatoes. "Can't have no ham without tomatoes, Ma."

Mrs. Watson turned toward me. "Now you eat up, sonny. Looks like you need a good woman to feed you right."

Jenny glanced at the empty place setting, the empty seat. She spooned out some ham and green beans on my plate and handed me a biscuit. Soon a slice of tomato adorned my plate, and then we started on the corn. Eating corn on the cob was not a delicate matter. It was somewhat messy, but I enjoyed chewing across the rows of kernels that were soaked in butter and salt. Jenny kept her little finger poised upward while holding each cob as if to add some form of grace.

Mrs. Watson was scraping the corn off the cob onto her plate. "What you want to know 'bout that ole fool, Francis, anyhow."

I set down an empty cob. "I'm not sure. He killed my father, but something just doesn't seem right."

Mrs. Watson pointed her fork across the table at her husband. "Tell him 'bout the nickel or a dime."

I looked at Mr. Watson. He waved his hand. "Later, after supper."

After we were done, I offered to help with the dishes, but both Mrs. Watson and Jenny quickly cleared the table with the exception of the fifth place setting. Mrs. Watson turned toward Jenny. "He'll be along soon, sugar."

Mr. Watson stood and patted his round belly. "Let's get us some fresh air, James."

I asked Mrs. Watson again if I could help, but she simply pushed me out of her kitchen while stating that guests don't work in her kitchen.

Out on the porch, Mr. Watson and I sat on the lounger. The bottle clinked against the metal frame behind the lounger. He was kind enough to offer me the first hit of booze. I could only see his pale, round face in the dim light coming from the a veiled window nearby. After a swig, I handed back the bottle by simply touching it to his chest. After he took his drink, we watched the fireflies that sprinkled the darkness with hope. It was so amazingly dark there. I had forgotten how dark it was at night in the country. I was used to the ever-present glow of the city that ignored the beauty of these tiny entities fluttering about the darkness as if moths which contained their own light.

He handed me the bottle again. "So, you want to hear 'bout the nickel and dime?"

I said yes.

"Seems them college kids was always botherin' Francis…in a nice kinda way. He wasn't exactly right you know. Walked around with an ax." The tree frogs started a gentle chirping just to the left of the farm.

"I know. We used to sneak up on him when we were kids."

"Never hurt you though." The sprinkling of light from the fireflies was quelled by two headlights beaming onto the property and then up the hill. "That'd be Mathis." The car pulled around to the back of the house. "Anyway, they always played the same trick on 'im, kinda tradition. They'd hold a dime in one hand and a nickel in the other and tell Francis he could have one or the other." He handed me the bottle.

"And?"

He laughed. "Francis always took the nickel. Tree frogs gettin' louder. 'Spect it's gonna rain tonight."

"I don't understand."

"I didn't either."

The tree frogs were louder, almost frantic in their chorus. "Why did he always take the nickel?"

Mr. Watson stood. "Had to ask him one day. Said if he took the dime, them college boys would stop playin'."

I stood as well and wandered about the porch for awhile. "I should thank Mrs. Watson for the meal."

"You just did. I'll tell her."

I paused at the porch steps. "So Francis--"

"Wasn't no dummy, smarter than you think."

He told me that I was always welcome to come pick some corn or tomatoes and wished me good night. I walked into the darkness trying to find my car while the fireflies danced about me to the rhythm of the trees frogs. The rhythm increased. I caught a firefly with my hand, and after it glowed in my open palm, it fluttered away to join the rest of the chorus. I could smell the rain coming.

I felt safer after my car started...from what I don't know. The headlights seemed like tiny tunnels of light along the country road. The tree frogs chirped so loudly, as if inside my head, chirping faster and faster. Each turn of the black road seemed like an invitation to an unknown place. The chirping grew louder and louder. Large drops

of rain pounded the windshield, and I thought I saw a
gray figure walking across the road with an ax. I pushed
the brake petal. There was a loud thump, then gravel
under the tires. I stepped out of the car, now jackknifed in
the road. Screaming, a woman was screaming in pain.
The rain soaked me, and she was lying there next to the
road pushing me away, kicking at me, the horrible
screams. Lights, red and blue, flashing. Bright lights, I
couldn't see. A thick hand pulled me away.

"Easy now." At first, all I could make out was the
silhouette of large man. She still screamed. He walked me
back to his car. "Jenny, you know how to drive a stick?
He's a bit shook up."

"Mathis, you know I been drivin' that old pick-up
most my life."

"Reckon you need a lift."

I looked at his pudgy face. "We need to save her."
I started to pull away from him.

"Once they start screamin' like that, ain't nothin'
nobody can do." He sat me in the car and walked over to
the body. Then I heard a loud gunshot. He returned to the
car.

"What did you do?" I asked.

"She ain't feelin' no pain now." He turned off the
flashing lights of the police cruiser. "Where're you
stayin'?" I could barely make out his face in the dim
light. I told him where. He pulled in front of Jenny who
was now in my car, and then I saw blood-soaked deer
next to the road. "Happens all the time. Hit a possum
'bout every night seems like. You're lucky that she was a
small one, not your fault." The rain beat down on the
windshield, almost defeating the efforts of the wipers.
"Deer 'round here are out a control. Huntin' season's
comin' up. Hate when they scream like that."

"It was a deer?"

He laughed. "Yeah, what'd you think it was, some
ghost or somethin'?" He drove on, showed me a shortcut
down a dirt road. Then we crossed a small stream and
drove up a winding, steep hill that looked familiar. "Why
did the chicken cross the road?"

"What?" I asked.

"Exactly, never seen no dead chicken in the road.
Reckon we should know why the deer crossed the road."
His laughter filled the car, almost drowning out the large
pellets of rain slapping the car.

"Steve, we got 'nother sitiation with Harold,"
came through the speaker.

Mathis picked up the hand set. "Same spot?"

"Ten four."

"Get Paul over there. I'll be along shortly." The
drive back started to seem longer than the drive out to the
Watsons' place. "Hear you're lookin' into that ole fool
Francis."

My hands had just stopped shaking, but the way
Mathis said that started them up again. "Yes. Killed my
father and--"

"My best friend." Then I realized that this was
Steve Mathis sitting next to me, my little brother's best
friend in elementary school. He pulled up to the Motel 3,
and I could barely make out his face in the dim light
coming from the dashboard. "You'd be best off to just
leave this be. Won't do nobody no good, 'specially you.
My Daddy told me all 'bout what done happened back
then when he's sheriff."

"Was I there?"

He turned and faced me. "Let it be, James."

"I don't…"

"Go on now, get some rest." He handed me his
card after writing his home number on the back. I stepped
out of the car and held the door open for Jenny. She
handed the keys to me. I thanked them both for their help,

and they drove away after wishing me a good evening and inviting me out for a drink sometime.

I walked slowly toward my room despite the drenching rain. It may have been the booze or a full meal or just a long, troubling day, but I only remember hearing the metal springs of the bed creak before I was awakened by a loud truck the next morning.

Asylum

I thought about the whole thing during the drive
back to D.C. Who would my lame investigation in
Picketsville actually help? Yet, it gnawed at me like the
growing pains that I felt as a child, the relentless pains of
my bones changing and growing. I was worried about
Oliver, and I so much wanted to see Robin. Given our
lack of contact, I worried that she might have found
someone else or perhaps had reconciled with her
husband.

My little townhouse was still there, and the
electric garage door opener rattled the door up. I could
hear Oliver's meows before I stepped out of the car.
Inside, he was quite vocal as usual upon my arrival, and I
immediately checked his food and water upstairs in the
kitchen. They were fine, but that really wasn't the point
for him. I dumped out the day-old food and water and
replaced them with a fresh batch. He immediately took a
few bites of his dry food. I then grabbed a few aspirin and
a cold beer to soften my hangover from my visit with the
Watsons, and he followed me into the living room. The
house felt stuffy, congested. So I opened up a few
windows and the deck door to let in the moist, summer
air.

Robin's voicemail at her office said that she would
call right back. I almost didn't leave a message, but did so
despite my fear that she might not return my call. After
playing with Oliver for awhile, I took my travel bag
upstairs. Susan was not in the bedroom, but the Lion was
curled up in the corner snoring, his long whiskers
quivering every so often. It seemed best not to wake him,
and I removed Cynthia's presents from the bag and went
downstairs.

In the kitchen, I popped another beer and reviewed the options for dinner in the freezer and in the cabinets. I heard Mark's laugh through the deck door. "Don't worry about it." I heard him say. "What's a little gas? The sluts won't know the difference." I quietly walked closer to the door. "Tonight, same place?" He must have hung up the phone or walked back into his house. The word, gas, seemed odd in that context.

After finishing the beer, I went downstairs and changed Oliver's litter. Something about the smell of the fresh litter disturbed me. The odor was different somehow, reminded me of something. I sat down at the computer and tried to write for awhile, but nothing seemed to work. The disturbing smell of the fresh litter and Mark's strange conversation dominated my thoughts, which were occasionally further distracted by the unsettling tone that Mathis had used when telling me to leave the past alone.

I shut down the computer and went back upstairs. While I stood gazing at Cynthia's gifts and at the empty notebooks that I had bought along with them, the doorbell rang. When I opened the door, a strong breeze blew through the house from the open deck door, and there stood Stone in his beat-up, tan blazer and un-pressed, black slacks. He didn't say a thing as he walked up the stairs. I offered him a seat mostly because watching him walk with his limp was somewhat disturbing. He declined.

"Where were you yesterday?" he asked while I went to the kitchen for his ashtray.

"I went to my hometown in southern Virginia." I set the ashtray on the pine coffee table.

He was flipping through my CD's. "I told you not to leave town." He turned and peered at me with his dark eyes. "Maybe I should lock you up."

I sat in my black leather chair. "I was only gone for a day."

"That's not the point." His voice was almost fatherly, as if I were a child being scolded.

"I'm doing research there. Maybe I can just let you know when I go?" I sipped my beer.

He flipped a CD against another, the plastic cases making a soft click. "Hmm, you need more jazz in your collection." He wandered across the room.

"Well, your wardrobe needs a bit of work."

"What's this?" He pointed at the dining room table. "Did you buy some presents for me?"

"Sure, if you like coloring books." He pulled out a cigarette and fumbled to find some matches. I went to the kitchen and brought back a book of matches. He had moved the ashtray to the end table where I realized I had hidden the plate of coke in the drawer.

"I prefer connect the dots." He tapped the butt of the cigarette on his thumbnail as usual. "What sort of research?" He lit his smoke.

"My father's death." I was trying to figure out a way to get Stone away from the table, away from the coke.

He blew some smoke out through his nostrils, which seemed to almost envelop his face. "I'm sorry to hear that."

The poignant odor from the match sulfur made me sneeze. "It's not your fault. Besides it's been awhile since he was murdered." I was relieved when he walked across the room, despite his awkward limp. He asked about the murder of my father, and I told him what little I knew, particularly that I did not trust the investigation at the time. "Maybe you can help me with it. I can't seem to find the court records."

He finally sat down on the couch. "I solve one murder at a time."

I set my empty beer can on the coffee table. "Yes,
I was wondering what brought you here this afternoon."
He leaned forward. "A confession would be nice."
His ever-frowning lips curled slightly upward.

"Then we wouldn't have these delightful chats."

"I'll come visit you in jail."

I laughed. "Sounds like you're stuck."

"I'll get the killer. I always do." He put out his
cigarette.

I stood. "I'm going to have another beer. Care for
one?" He waved his hand. I walked out into the kitchen.
"Afraid the only other options are soda or tea." He said
that a soda would be nice. I popped it open and set the
can and a glass on the table in front of him. He ignored
the glass, took a sip, and then started to tap another
cigarette on his thumbnail.

"Sure you can't tell me anything else about your
wife?"

"I miss her." The phone rang. I quickly picked it
up hoping that it was Robin returning my call.

"Mr. Douglas?"

"Yes." I figured I would now be advised how
toget a better mortgage rate by answering a few
questions.

"Mr. James Douglas?"

I almost hung up. "This is Karen McConnel,
Sandy's sister." She went on to apologize for not
attending the funeral, and I expressed my remorse for her
loss. I watched Stone sipping his soda.

"Her things are still here, and I want you and your
family to have whatever you want." I looked at Stone's
pack of cigarettes and curiously wanted one.

"Have they found the killer yet?"

"The detective in charge is sitting right here." I
handed the phone to Stone. I smiled.

He frowned and took the phone. While they were talking, I noticed that the stereo and books needed to be dusted. "Suspect," he said. "I may be very close to one even while we speak." He offered a small grin when I looked at him. After he handed the phone back to me, I told her to let me know when she would like to go through Sandy's things. She thanked me and stated that she would be in touch soon.

Stone pulled his leg closer to the couch. "Seemed like a nice young lady."

I stood, my beer now empty. "What about Kevin Brown?"

While I was in the kitchen, Stone said, "Neither one of you has a decent alibi, and you both had motive."

I walked back in with a fresh beer. "What's my motive?"

"Jealousy."

"I didn't know about Kevin."

"Yeah right." He stood "You always drink this much so early in the day?"

"I have a headache. Detectives stopping by without calling first may be the cause."

He limped toward the door. "You'll just have a headache again tomorrow."

I wished him well, and after locking the door behind him, I immediately poured the coke down the sink. I then sat for awhile hoping that the phone would ring. Sandy's sister had sounded very professional on the phone, almost matter of fact with only an occasional hint in her tone that her sister's death upset her. I was somewhat relieved that she had called. I knew it would be healthy to get rid of Sandy's things, and felt that her family should have what was left of her existence here.

I ate a frozen dinner and then went down to the office and paid the pile of bills, many of which were late, and faced the awful truth about the damage that my sabbatical from the computer industry had rendered upon my finances. I also discovered that it was too late to register for a fall semester class, but that seemed for the best given the various distractions in my life. Despite the waning sunlight, I decided that washing my car might clear my mind. The parents were rounding up their children for the night, and the kids scampered after their balls and skates. A few of the neighbors walked by and expressed their condolences about Sandy and how nice a person she was. This didn't really help much, but it was nice of them to acknowledge her absence. In fact, I wanted to forget the whole thing and move on, but it seemed that no one was interested in letting me do so.

Mark startled me while I was drying my car off. "Hey, Man."

I turned around. He was sporting a red, Maryland tee shirt. "Go Turtles," I said.

"Go Turtles. She looks nice." He grabbed the other towel and helped with the drying. "Can you give me a lift somewhere? Won't take long."

I started to say no. "For what?"

"Need to drop something off." He tossed the dirty, pink towel across the hood of the car.

I thought about it while I gathered the sponges and the bucket. "Why not. When?"

"I'm ready now."

"Give me a few minutes." I put the cleaning things back in their place in the garage and walked upstairs to grab my money clip and exchange my flip-flops for some tennis shoes. After I wiped the sweat off my face and under arms, I went back outside. Mark was already in the car. He had opened the sunroof and was playing around with the radio dial.

I got in. "Where to?" He told me the general direction. As we drove along, I wondered why I had agreed. Then the evening air blowing across the sunroof and into the windows as we cruised along the highway reminded me of cruising at night along the back roads of Picketsville when I was much younger with a the sense that anything could happen and that only this night existed. We pulled up to the apartment complex where I had dropped off Jamie the day before, and Mark picked up a brown paper bag off the floor.

"I'll be right back." He walked through the dark parking lot, his shadow occasionally appearing beneath the street lights. Then he was gone.

I lay my head back and gazed up at the milky haze of the city glow in the sky. I couldn't find any stars, and the oppressive heat of August seemed to rise as much from the pavement as from the soggy, motionless air around me.

While I watched the moths beat themselves against a nearby streetlight, Mark opened the door and hopped in. "Get going, Man." I looked at him. "Go." I pulled out of the parking lot. He still had a brown paper bag in his hand. I checked the review mirror, and there sat Susan. I almost swerved off the road.

She smiled. "Keep one hand on the road, James."

"One hand?"

"What?" asked Mark.

"Home, James." Susan said with a chuckle.

"I'll take you home, bitch." I down shifted and accelerated.

"Who are you calling a bitch? It's party time, Man." The street lamps flashed by until we arrived safely back at my place. Susan walked into the garage and waved. Mark insisted that I come to his place for a bit.

He told me to grab the tequila and a lemon out of the refrigerator and went upstairs. After slicing the lemon, I set the bottle and lemon slices on the glass coffee table in the living room and sat on the puffy, white couch where I had performed sex with Jamie for Mark's entertainment. He came down the stairs and set a scale on the table and pulled what appeared to be at least a couple ounces of coke out of the brown paper bag.

"Go Turtles." He picked up the bottle and took a long drink. "To hell with the salt." He handed it to me. I resisted his offer for lines of coke, but it was becoming more and more difficult with each shot.

He was almost done cutting and bagging the coke into smaller packets when we finished the bottle. "Oops." I held the bottle up. Then I grabbed a slice of lemon.

"Hey, think I don't have another bottle?" He gathered the smaller packets and the scale and took them upstairs. I stared at the large pile he had left on the table. He returned with another bottle and started to hand me a packet with a few grams. "Thanks for the loan, Man."

"I really don't--"

"Do it with Jamie." He pushed it into my shirt pocket.

"Go turtles." He took a shot.

"Here's to Francis the Ax Man." I took a shot and then stood up. It seemed as though someone was tilting the floor back and forth while I walked to the bathroom.

I awoke late the next morning on Sandy's couch, my left arm numb from having my dead weight on it too long. Stone had been right. I still had a headache which became much worse when I sat up. My mouth was so dry that I could hardly move my tongue, and the cracks in my parched lips hurt while I choked down some water. I sat in my chair nursing a bottle of water, holding an ice pack against my forehead. I couldn't recall how I returned home or if I had finally given in to Mark's offers to do a few lines. Then I remembered the packet that Mark had shoved into my pocket. I pulled it out and stared at the rich man's aspirin thinking how quickly it would numb me from everything. I opened it and dabbed some onto

my finger and tasted it. It quickly numbed my tongue. I
started to go look for something to pour it on when I
realized the connection between Mark's reference to gas
and the taste in my mouth.

I paced for a few minutes. Then I called Stone. I
had to be aggressive to find out that he was at home for
the day looking after his wife and to get them to patch me
through to him. They finally did after I explained that I
had to speak with him, having used the word, emergency,
several times. He gave me directions to his house. I took
a shower and drove to his place in Rockville.

It was an old neighborhood with large trees and
large houses with tastefully groomed yards, well
groomed, but not to the obscene extent of hedges cut in
patterns or statues of naked boys peeing into bird baths. I
pulled under the large oak trees that draped stone's
driveway and yard in a curiously protective manner. I
walked around to the back of the single-story, red-brick
house as he had instructed. Stone was kneeling next to a
slate patio. He was wearing blue overalls and a brown tee
shirt and was pulling weeds from between the purple
petunias. He looked up and slowly stood up.

"Well, it's good that you stopped by. I can use a
little help with the mulch." He pointed the hand-sized
rake at the bags of mulch next to the driveway. Then I
saw a woman seated in a wheelchair trimming the juniper
bushes on the opposite side of the patio. "That's Mrs.
Stone. Mother Stone, here's that murderer I was telling
you about." She looked up, her head tilted to her right and
waved the trimmers at me with her left hand. Her
colorless eyes didn't seem to look at me. Her yellow,
almost orange, hair was cut short and held away from her
angular, sunken face with bobby pins. In spite of the heat,
she had a blue afghan draped over her legs, and her
blouse, an off-white color, seemed more like a nightshirt.

"Mrs. Stone, I'm sorry to disturb you here," I said.
"It's a beautiful day to be out caring for the yard." I could
tell that in addition to the wheelchair, something else was
also wrong. Her hands moved very slowly, and each cut
of a bush branch appeared to be a contest of her will
against her body to do so.

Stone started to hobble toward the bags of mulch.
"Come on. Make yourself useful."

I tapped his shoulder. "I'll bring them over.
Maybe Mrs. Stone needs something cold to drink."

He turned around. "I suppose I could use a rest."
As it turns out, he did know how to smile. He seemed
smaller, yet more alive, out tending to his yard with his
wife. While I dragged the bags of mulch over to the patio,
I watched him kiss her on the forehead and say something
to her. She waved the clippers at him, and he laughed.
After I had placed the last bag next to the patio, Stone and
I began to cover the surrounding garden with the mulch.

"This is a Japanese maple." He awkwardly
squatted and spread the mulch that I had poured around
its base.

"It's beautiful." I tossed the empty bag into the
pile.

"She had a stroke a few years ago. Red leaves
instead of green. It adds a bit of color. Of course, they'll
all be red and yellow soon." He stood and limped back
toward the house. "Let's get something cold to drink, and
you can tell me about your emergency." We walked into
the house. I asked if Mrs. Stone would be all right, and he
advised me that it was just about the time when the birds
came to feed. "Watching the birds and trimming those
bushes seem to be her only joys." He pointed toward the
kitchen. "She's not very happy when winter comes." He
poured two glasses of lemonade and then led me to his
study. It was a large room with book shelves built into
dark, mahogany walls. Almost all of the books were hard

cover, and there were various pictures from the police academy and from his military service. One wall displayed only Civil War rifles. He didn't apologize for the dust or the papers that were strewn across his maple desk. I felt quite confident that if I asked, he would tell me that he knew exactly where everything was. He sat behind it and pointed to a chair on the other side.

I sat in the matching maple chair. "Good lemonade."

"Home made." He removed his holstered gun from the top of the desk and placed it in a drawer. "So tell me. What is so urgent?"

"I'm sorry to bother you at home." I looked for a coaster on his desk without success. "I think some people are in trouble." He pushed a yellow memo pad across the desk, and I set the drink on it. I stood and pulled the coke out of my jeans and handed it to him. He took it. "It's cocaine."

"Yes, drugs are bad. Why--"

"Taste it." I sat down.

He looked at me, and I suppose he was trying to figure out whether or not to have me taste it first. He tucked his finger into the bag and then licked it. After a moment, "yes, it's coke."

"What else do you taste?" He stood up and looked out the window. He pointed. I stood and saw Mrs. Stone tossing bird seed onto the patio, and all different sorts of birds hopped about the patio pecking at the seeds. We both sat.

"I don't understand."

"Kitty litter. That's what we used to call it back when I was stupid enough to snort this crap. It tastes like kitty litter."

"I've never tasted kitty litter." He set the bag on the desk. "You know I should just charge you with possession, maybe with intent."

"Why would I come here with it? It's been tainted, probably with gasoline during shipment."

"How would you know?" He took a handkerchief out of his pocket and mopped the sweat off his forehead.

"There was a batch of coke that tasted just like this that was being distributed almost a decade ago." My palms felt moist. "It killed a lot of people." The chirping of the birds outside sounded like a gang of high-school girls at a party. "The rumor was that a shipment of coke was spoiled by gasoline during shipment, but the pricks sold it anyway."

"What do you want from me?" He picked the packet up again.

"I know who is selling it, at least one of the people." I gulped down the rest of the lemonade. I then told him about Mark and the parking lot where Mark bought the coke.
"Have your lab test it."

He sealed the packet and set it on the desk. "This doesn't change anything regarding your wife's murder."

"I understand, but maybe you can help me find out more about my father's death."

He told me that he would see what he could do and walked me out.

During the ride home, my stomach felt queasy and gurgled from a lack of food. I wasn't sure if it was sweat from the August heat or the alcohol pouring out through the pores in my skin, but I was soaked when I arrived home. I sat in the living room and ate some canned, fruit cocktail hoping that my stomach might not reject it. Afterward, I took a cold shower, turned on the fan next to my bed and lay down for a nap.

Sandy's body slides out of the drawer, naked, her skin partially eaten by maggots and hideous insects. Her

lovely breasts cut and mangled, and her loins torn,
bloody. Her eyes twitch. Her cracked lips are sewn shut.
The pillow and the sheets were soaked in my
sweat. I wiped the drool from my cheek and went
downstairs for some water. There was none left. I drank
some tap water and then went back upstairs with an ice
pack for my throbbing head. There were three bottles of
cold water on my bureau. I swore to never drink tequila
again if I could just rest for awhile, sleep without
nightmares. The dreams were acute throughout the night,
and I woke almost every ninety minutes, my face and
pillow covered in sweat. The Lion kept me company,
purring me back to sleep. His fur felt soft and well
groomed.

The next day, I realized that I had slept, off and
on, for almost fifteen hours. I felt much better, my head
no longer throbbing. My stomach seemed capable of
keeping down anything that I had a taste for, as long as it
was soon. I picked up a corn beef sandwich from the deli
down the street and finished it while waiting at a traffic
light on the way home.
Back at home, I updated my journal, particularly
the part about Picketsville. Then I noticed that I had a
voice mail. It was Robin. I was delighted to hear her say
that Cynthia couldn't wait to see Oliver and Chef James.
But Robin went on to state that she thought it would be
best for us not to see each other for awhile longer and that
I needed to go back to see Dr. Fowler. I deleted the
message and almost threw the phone across the room.
Despite the darkening sky, I went outside to weed
our little flower gardens and check the supports for the
deck. The wasps had returned, and I took some of my
anger and frustration out on them with bug spray and a
hose. I then decided to use the rage, to cathartically purge
it by writing more about my rapist character.

After I finished killing a girl who looked a bit like
Sandy, I returned to the living room. Oliver followed me
while I paced back and forth from the living room to the
kitchen, trying to remind me with all his cutest moves and
best verbal skills that his stomach, like mine, was
growling. I fed him and then sat down and looked
through the various delivery menus. Pizza won the
contest. I flipped on the news and was immediately
bombarded with pharmaceutical ads. The side affects of
the medicine seemed worse than the illness. Then my
favorite ad came on which boasted a cure for Generalized
Anxiety Disorder. It always made me laugh since it
seemed that the drug could be legitimately sold to
everyone on the planet. Who doesn't have some anxiety
in their life? I thought. Then there were the side affects:
diarrhea, vomiting, dry mouth, loss of sleep and
impotence. It seemed to me that those would be the types
of things that would give a person general anxiety. The
doorbell rang.

"Hey, Man." Steam from the recent thunderstorm
rose from the black pavement behind Mark.

I invited him in. "I'm kind of busy right now.
What's up?"

He seemed a bit anxious and sat on the couch. His
black hair was matted and oily. or perhaps sweaty. His
dark pupils seemed to fill all but a tiny sliver of the white
in his eyes. "What did you do with that eight ball I gave
you?"

I hadn't thought of this possibility. "I sold it." I sat
in my chair.

"Think you can sell some more?" There was
sweat beading up on his forehead. His face was pale.

"That's probably not a good idea. Besides I'm kind
of busy with my writing."

"About the rapist, right?"

121

I leaned forward. "How did you…"

"Relax, Man. Your secret is safe with me. You were tore up the other night. Jamie helped me carry you home," he said.

I picked up a pen and started to twirl it in and out of my fingers. "The secret about my book?"

"No, Man. About how you killed that cheating wife of yours, strangled her at the Metro stop with her pink, silk scarf." He pulled out a glass vial and a little spoon and did a couple snorts.

I started to stand, but my knees were limp. I stared at him. He offered the vial to me. I waved my hand. "I said I killed her?"

He put the cap back on the vial. "Don't worry about it. It's cool."

"Are you sure?"

"Yeah. You said you took a silver, pearl-drop earring as a souvenir."

"I…"

"Hey, I'd probably do the same thing." He stood. "Well, I better go sell the rest of this before the girls do it all." He walked to the foyer. "Go Turtles." With that he was gone.

I don't remember what the pizza delivery person looked like or even if I had given him or her a tip. I walked around the living room holding the pizza for awhile, its alluring aroma teasing my twisting stomach. I threw it into the kitchen, sat, stood, paced, went into the kitchen and started cleaning it up off the floor. It made no sense, telling Mark of all people. Then again, I had passed out. I had already concluded that I was capable of murder. Otherwise I would not have been able to develop a character who was capable of such violence. Rage, confusion and fear yielded to a numbing fatigue.

I sat on the deck for awhile. The frolicking birds darting overhead and then perching on the trees and rooftops offered little solace, and the flowers, moist from the rain, waved gently in the warm breeze as if nothing had happened. Susan sat next to me wearing one of Sandy's summer dresses. She giggled and waved her arms at the birds who chirped to her. She said nothing, just looked at me and nodded. I didn't have the energy to scold her for wearing Sandy's clothes. We watched the birds together while the evening sun slowly meandered through the puffy white clouds.

When the sun had set, and the birds had retired for the night, I resisted the temptation to get drunk and went to bed and tried to sleep.

The lights are out at the Shady Grove Metro stop, uncomfortable, dark, like out in the country where Dad lives.

Mother chops the onions with vigorous pops against the cutting board

"Don't ever speak to your mother like that." Dad throws me against the fake-wood wall. The nail holding the calendar pokes into the back of my head. The calendar flutters into the air.

The calendar smacks against the floor, and then Dad throws me across the room onto my little brother. Steve yelps and lies still.

Mother charges with a knife. The screaming.

We're in the pasture now. She lays Steve's body next to Dad's. "Go get his ax."

His shack has vines on it, cans and pots. I run down the hill to Mother with the ax.

She takes the ax from me and sinks it into father's chest, the bones snapping, popping like small branches on a tree. The popping, the red.

"I can't do that to my own son." She hands me the ax.

Steve is peaceful. I swing, more popping.
"Again." Snapping. My hands are red. I can't see them
now. The ax is on the ground.

I woke on the floor, then fumbled through the
darkness. My heart pounded such that I thought it might
leave my chest, but I was thankful to have my hands. I
managed to simply crawl back into the bed. I felt the Lion
next to me.

"You're just like me," he said.

"I am?" I could only see a dark silhouette against
cracks of orange light from the streetlamps slipping
around the curtains.

He licked my head and ears and then rubbed his
whiskers against my cheek. "Look at my life."

"Sleeping a lot?"

"I sleep well, not like you."

"Why?"

"I have no conscience. I just survive. I kill, eat
and get laid as a matter of right. It's my job. Total
clarity."

"What should I do?"

He started a low and soft purring. "What's most
efficient?"

"Kill Mark."

"There you go. Rest now."

Mark had all but convinced me that I had
murdered my wife. To a certain extent, this added clarity
to my thoughts. I slowly distilled the various options with
the help of Susan and the Lion who acted like advocates
on opposite sides of the issue. Susan pushed the need for
redemption, and she insisted that I confess. To this I
argued that I was not completely sure that I had killed
Sandy. The Lion of course advocated survival, that there
was no point in my going to jail. To that end, he
reminded me of the difficulties regarding Mark. I had to

agree with him. Given normal circumstances, Mark would probably not report me. He would rather blackmail me in some way, and a confession from one drunk to another wasn't all that compelling. The problem stemmed from the fact that I had reported his drug dealing to Stonc. It seemed logical that he would turn me in if he knew that I had done so, or if it bought him a better sentence. We adjourned with the Lion having convinced me to at least investigate ways of killing Mark.

Over the next few days, I did just that. But I did it through the character in my novel. After all, he was an experienced and accomplished serial killer. I wrote how he might do it, how to plan it. One fundamental problem remained despite his various plans. Both He and Mark might be under police surveillance. There just didn't seem to be a way around it.

I then decided that I hadn't killed her. This was mostly a matter of convenience given the other solutions. Although, given that I was debating such issues with a ghost and a lion and that sleep remained such an unwelcome place, I scheduled an appointment with Dr. Fowler for the following week.

Later that day, Stone called with some information regarding my father's death. He said that all he could come up with was the name and address of a retired professor who his source said might know something. "There's not much else I can find," he went on to say.

"I appreciate it."

"I suppose you'll want to go there and talk to him?"

"Yes."

"All right. Let me know when you're going, and you need to check in with me every day. Don't make me come looking for you."

"I understand. What happened with that other thing?"

"Stay away from Mark. That's all I can tell you."

Harvest

The following day, I called Stone and left a message with the phone number for the Motel 3 in Picketsville and stated that I might be gone for a couple of days. Oliver was upset because he knew I was packing for a trip. I packed extra clothes, almost enough for a week, and I put the couple of thousand that I kept as an emergency stash in the bag as well.

I left the radio off and enjoyed the morning breeze whistling through the sunroof and windows as I cruised along the back roads toward Picketsville. My thoughts slowly began to settle, and I focussed only on Francis the Ax Man and Professor Steiner while I drove deeper into the country. Soon there were large, open fields, many with huge combines mowing down the endless rows of corn, pieces of the stalks violently flying up in the air, the unwanted pieces that would fertilize next year's crop, a sacrifice for the greater good.

I asked directions to Steiner's place from a produce vendor after buying a few peaches. He lived on the north side of town in a little, brick apartment next to the hospital, his second to last stop on his way to the grave. It took awhile for him to open the door. He looked half the size I recalled and seemed happy to have a visitor.

"Come on in," he said. He hobbled over to his pale-green recliner and pulled a pink and blue afghan over his wobbly legs. "I know why you came."

"Oh?" I wasn't sure if I should sit unless invited to.

He rubbed his narrow chin and then ran his hand across his short, gray hair that appeared to stand up due to static. "They might score." The team in the red shirts advanced the soccer ball toward the goal and kicked it wide. The TV flickered.

"Someone said you could tell me what happened to my father."

"They did huh? Well, adjust the antenna. The game's fading." I pulled one of the rods forward. "No, the other one." I tried it, but as soon as I let go, the picture fuzzed away. "Just hold it. The game's almost over, none of those bullshit timeouts like in football." I stood holding the antenna. "I was there."

"What?" I said.

"It's nice to have a visitor." He started to raise up out of the recliner. "I think I might have some cookies."

"Please don't trouble yourself."

"Mrs. Johnson keeps bringing by cookies." His voice crackled. He winked at me. "She has a thing for me you know."

I smiled but let go of the antenna.

"You stole his ax that day. Now grab that rabbit ear so I can finish the game."

"What?"

"You would be best off to go on back to Maryland and forget this whole thing. No point. Might not like what you find. I have some cookies, oatmeal, I think."

I shook my head and then stood there for a moment holding the antenna while Steiner watched his game. The whistle blew, and the match ended in a tie. He turned off the TV and looked at me with his light-gray eyes. "You're not going to let this go are you?"

I realized that I was still holding the antenna and let go of it. "I can't."

"Go out in the kitchen and bring in those cookies sitting on the counter." I did and returned with a plate of cookies covered in a clear wrap. I handed it to him. I declined his offer for one. "Mathis is who you need to talk to."

"Steve?"

"Mathis Senior, not that nitwit boy of his." He waved a half-eaten cookie at me. "Watch him, and don't let him talk you into playing poker."

He finally offered me a seat, and I ate a couple of cookies with him while he told me a few stories about how he and my father used to argue and raise hell with each other at the faculty meetings. I soon realized that I was not going to get any more out of him. He insisted on seeing me to the door, despite the fact that it was only a few feet away from his chair. I asked him to wait at the door, and I returned from my car and gave him the peaches that I had just bought.

He smiled. "You know the World Cup is coming up. Come on down if you get bored up there in D.C. Besides, you're a good antenna holder." He laughed. I wished him well. Driving out to the main road, I thought about how the last thing that D.C was to me was boring. In fact, I wanted it to get boring.

I drove over to the Motel 3 and checked in, receiving the same red-carpet treatment as the last time--a grimace and a groan from the little man behind the desk. He gave me the same wonderful room with no phone. I went to the pay phone at the corner of the building and called Mathis Junior. His office relayed the call to his squad car, and I soon had a lunch date with both him and Jenny.

I followed his directions to the Red Lion Inn and met them outside. I hadn't really been able to get a good look at him the last time I was in Picketsville. He had a bear-like physique with neatly cut, blond hair that matched his eyebrows that had little stray strands which stuck out over his dark-green eyes. He was wearing blue overalls and a white tee shirt which amplified the pink tone of his face and arms. He greeted me with a smile,

and we went into the restaurant and sat at the table that
Jenny had already secured. It was incredibly dark inside.
The majority of the light came from little candles on the
tables. A waiter soon came over to the table.

"You like burgers?" Mathis asked.

"Sure," I said.

"Three third-pound burgers and fries," he told the
waiter.

Jenny excused herself to the ladies' room. Mathis
leaned forward, and in the flickering light, his head
appeared to be simply floating over the table. "Reckon
you're here 'bout your Daddy."

"I just spoke with Professor Steiner."

"And?"

"He said I need to speak with your father."

Mathis' head floated back away from the table.
"Reckon we just gonna have to deal with this. So be it."

"I'm not trying to cause any trouble for you. I just
have to…it's making me crazy."

Mathis chuckled. "And most folks ain't even got
an excuse for that."

Suddenly Jenny was sitting next to me. "He tellin'
you about his huntin' yesterday?"

"Hush, girl." His voice was gruff.

"Got him a big ole squirrel. He's lucky he had his
rifle 'cause that squirrel was mighty big, could a killed
'im."

I couldn't really see his face, but I thought that it
was probably growing pinker beyond the burn from the
sun. "We better call the local sheriff and tell him about
these giant squirrels," I said.

There was a pregnant pause, and then Mathis
started laughing. It sounded hearty and genuine. Jenny
and I joined in. "Well, that's why we're eatin' burgers
today," he said. "Best burger anywhere."

He was right. It was a good burger, and I thought that the waiter must have used a wheel barrow to bring them out to the table. We ate in silence mostly. Mathis talked a bit about my little brother, Steve.

"He looked up to you, James."

"I know." I choked down the last of my burger and chased it with a large gulp of beer.

Mathis' voice became soothing, like an officer trying to talk a jumper away from a ledge. "He'd a done anythin' for ya. I miss him. I know you do too."

"I--"

Jenny quickly injected, "Why don't you just come stay at our place? Got plenty a bedrooms."

"Save you a few bucks. Help us out in the fields. Be good for ya. You could use a touch of color." Mathis patted me on the back.

I offered some weak objections, but they solved all of them including Mathis saying that he would fix things at the Motel 3. I insisted on paying the check for lunch. Mathis objected of course, but my assurance that the next time would be on him gained his consent.

The light outside hurt my eyes at first. We got into our cars, and they followed me a few miles to the motel to collect my things. Mathis went to speak with Mr. Congeniality, and I threw my things into the car. I followed them down the windy back roads until just around a bend, Mathis stopped his car and flashed the police cruiser's lights. I pulled up behind them. Jenny hopped out and walked back and stepped into my car.

"He's gotta go deal with Harold again."

Mathis turned around, and Jenny and I drove on toward her place. We drove up the narrow driveway and stopped. I grabbed my bag, and we went into the house. She showed me to a large bedroom with a metal-framed bed and a dark-wood, antique bureau with a large mirror attached. The bed looked comfortable, particularly given how full I was from lunch. A nap seemed like a good idea. She instructed me to put on some shorts and left. In terms of pants, all I had were jeans and a pair of gym shorts that I wore when I slept. I had just put the shorts on when there was a knock at the door.

"Come in."

Jenny walked in with a large fan. "You'll need this tonight." She had changed into jean cut-offs and a red halter top. "Well I guess it's just you and me for the afternoon."

In an instant I took in her firm, tan legs and solid shoulders, and it was difficult to ignore the tops of her breasts.

I quickly put on a tee shirt. "Thank you."

"Everythin' okay in here? Bed okay?"

I smiled. "It's great."

"Good. Let's go have some fun."

I followed her with absolutely no idea what fun meant in this case. She led me out the backdoor to a field next to the corn where I was relieved that she had meant picking strawberries. She bent over and showed me the proper way to pick a strawberry and handed me a basket.

"There's a water pump up there case you get hot or thirsty." She pointed to it.

I thanked her, and we started on the first two rows. She was of course more efficient than me, but I enjoyed watching her bend over a few feet ahead of me. I engaged her in small talk for awhile. The strawberries were her project on the farm, and she took pride it. She had been dating Mathis for almost ten years, and she was clearly growing impatient.

I tried to change the subject quickly. "What emergency did he have to go to?"

"Harold."

"I don't understand."

She turned around. "Sad thing. His wife and him was in a car wreck while back. She died few days after." She bent over in front of me and plucked a strawberry, her breasts almost fully exposed and within my grasp. I turned away. "So what is the emergency now?" She kept picking the strawberries, and I kept trying to avoid looking at her breasts. "Like I said, sad thing. Thinks he killed her, responsible for it. He gets to drinkin', says he's a gonna kill himself. He only puts the gun down for Mathis."

I put another strawberry into the basket which topped it off. "That is sad."

We walked back and grabbed a couple more baskets. "Seen you lookin' at my breasts."

"I…"

"Oh don't blush." She handed me another basket. "Heck, I'd a been worried if you didn't look." She started walking back out into the field. I wiped the sweat off my face with the tail of my white tee shirt and followed. "Never did understand that."

"What?"

"Girls go fuss themselves up to look pretty and then get all mad if a man looks at 'em. Don't make no sense." She turned around and waved the basket. "I seen them prissy bitches with all their 'spensive clothes and hairdos act like you're 'spose to look but you can't or somethin', crazy. What's the point?"

"I don't know." We started picking again. "What if the man gets aroused. Is that fair?"

"He don't want to look, he don't have to." She pointed at the bulge in my shorts. "Guess we know you ain't one of them fag writers." She laughed.

I looked down, and while I wanted to think that my body was expressing admiration for her directness and honesty, it was expressing my almost uncontrollable visceral desires. "I'm sorry."

She smiled. "Looks like you got nothin' to be sorry 'bout."

"What if--"

"Mathis probably shoot ya."

I just stopped for a moment and tried to tuck my desire down or hide it better. Something buzzed past my ear. "Woo." Then something that looked like a bat darted up toward the cloudless sky.

"Oh. That's a purple martin, eats squiters." She stepped toward me and dropped a strawberry in my basket. "I'm sorry. I shouldn't otta be teasin' you like that."

I smiled. "Well, I never knew how fun picking strawberries could be."

We resumed the harvest. "Mathis' Daddy comin' over for supper tonight."

I looked up. "He is?"

"'Supposed to bring over some fish he caught." She started to pick the strawberries more quickly. "Momma 'spects all these to be in the house tonight so she can start makin' jam." I quickened my pace despite the sweat dripping from my face. "Guess the boys'll play poker, and me and Momma'll work on the cannin' again."

We hurried along. I focused my thoughts on Mathis holding a gun to my face instead of getting naked with Jenny and chasing her through the rows of corn. I also thought about what would happen with Mathis Senior, what he would tell me…or not tell me. We had filled several dozen baskets, and after we carried them all up to the back porch, we rinsed off at the rusty hand pump. I pumped for her and then she for me. I sat down on the back porch steps and lay my head back in exhaustion. A loud bang snapped me to my feet, and then another made me duck. I looked up, and there stood Jenny with a rifle.

"Damn crows. Too bad you can't eat 'em."

We went into the kitchen, and after Jenny poured
us both a large glass of ice tea, she asked about my
writing and about D.C. I lied. I told her that I was writing
a comedy, a play about a writer who becomes part of his
own play.
"I seen a few plays over at Jefferson. Can't say I
understood much."
"You're pretty sharp, Jenny."
"Can't compete with them D.C. girls, or ladies,"
she said with mocking frown.
"They don't have a thing on you. Just read more if
that's what you want."
She stood and freshened up our glasses. "What I
want is for Mathis to put a ring on this finger. I ain't
gettin' any younger, and Daddy wants a grandson."
The door opened and in walked Mathis. Jenny
stood and hugged him.
"How's Harold? she asked.
"Same." Mathis gave me a stern look. "He been
behavin'?"
"Yep, shame."
He started to tickle her around her naked belly
button. "What do you mean?"
She was laughing and started to return fire by
tickling his large belly. "He's a perfect gentleman, but
he's kinda cute. You know what pickin' them strawberries
can do."
"Well now, you must a missed a few. Reckon we
best go see."
They both looked at me. I was already smiling as
if I someone were tickling me too. I blinked both my eyes
in agreement and waved my hand. As Mathis pulled her
out the door, Jenny told me where to find the towels
should I wish to bathe. I was tempted to watch them, not
from some perversion, but more from a desire to witness
their joy in each other. I sat at the white, Formica-topped

table gulping down the ice tea to which Jenny had added what seemed to be just the right amount of ice cubes and lemon slices.

My thoughts unfortunately ventured into an internal debate about why I had not taken advantage of Jenny, or at least tried, why it felt good not to do so, and yet I had apparently murdered my wife, and according to Susan, had raped and killed her as well. What was different, I wondered. Had I changed, and if so why? I could smell the strawberries on my fingers, and feel the sun's work on my skin. I felt vibrantly alive and pleasantly exhausted. I went upstairs and lay down on the bed after turning on the fan and was quickly asleep.

Something shook beneath me, and I sat up. Mathis removed his hand from the bed and smiled. "Know a few girls that would be happy to take care of that for ya." I looked down and saw my erection trying to poke through my shorts. "Pickin' them strawberries can cause that to happen I hear."

"I didn't--"

"I know." He walked over and opened the curtains. "I'm just funin' ya."

I stood, picked up my jeans and put them on. I was tempted to ask him who might assist me with the tension in my shorts. It had been awhile. "I understand your father will be here for dinner."

He set a wash basin and a cloth on the bureau. "Kinda tradition, harvest time." He turned around and looked at me. "You'll see."

"Think he'll be angry with me for asking about Francis?"

He took out a red handkerchief and wiped the sweat off his eyebrows. "Steve was 'lergic to strawberries. I miss him." He walked toward the door. "A man should know how his Daddy died. That's for sure. We fixin' to get ready for supper." He closed the door.

I washed up, put on a shirt and walked downstairs and then into the kitchen. I asked Momma Watson if I could help, and she directed me to the pantry which was adjacent to the back porch. Jenny was inside cutting the tops off the strawberries.

"Well, guess we done wore you out today."

"I had fun. How can--"

She handed me a bowl of cut strawberries and pointed toward the spigot. I started to rinse them off. "You know, I got this girlfriend, real cute, might like ya. Name's Suzy." I dropped a couple of strawberries on the floor. "Them was the ones you picked, 'cause I'd have to get real mad if I picked 'em."

"I'm sorry."

"Don't worry yourself. Next time no nap though." She pointed the knife at me and grinned.

After she decided that we were done, we took them inside. Mrs. Watson labored over the stove, and despite the fact that I had eaten so much already that day, the smell of the fish made my stomach growl. I heard voices in the other room, and Jenny excused herself to freshen up. Mrs. Watson argued with me about my helping with dinner, but after I reminded her that she was providing not only a good meal but a comfortable bed, she instructed me on how to set the table.

After setting the table, I wandered out into the large house to find the voices and eventually found Watson and Mathis Senior in the living room.

"There he is," said Watson. He walked over to the bar and poured a drink and handed it to me. "Hear you was hell on them strawberries today." The other man had his back to me.

"Thank you. They can be contrary at times."

Watson laughed. "I guess you want to meet the great fisherman of Picketsville." The man turned around. His hair was gray, and he seemed like an older version of Mathis except that he was a bit thinner, and his eyes seemed weary. He was smartly dressed in cowboy boots, blue jeans, a black blazer and a dark-brown shirt. "This here is the real sheriff himself."

He finished his drink and handed his empty glass to Watson. He held out his hand, and I offered mine. He held his grip for a moment, his brown eyes staring into mine. He released. "Play poker?" It did not sound like a request.

"I play."

"That's good, that's good." He took the fresh drink from Watson and looked down at the floor. "Runnin' out of players these days. Seems like I'm buryin' a friend every week now."

Mrs. Watson interrupted our conversation by announcing that supper was ready. We finished our drinks, and I followed them into the kitchen. Jenny was already there wearing a lose, peach-colored, summer dress. We sat and Mrs. Watson placed a plate of grilled fish in the middle of the table. I ended up sitting next to Mathis Senior, across from Jenny and Junior, the Watsons at opposite ends of the table. Mrs. Watson passed around the corn bread and then the steaming ears of corn.

Mr. Watson looked at the table. "Thought you said you caught some big ins." He offered a sly grin to Mathis Senior. "I seen minnows bigger than these."

"Bull." Mathis Senior said. "You ain't caught fish since a fish caught you."

Mrs. Watson stood and started spooning out the cooked, string beans.

"At least it ain't squirrel." Jenny poked Mathis Junior in his side.

"Squirrel ain't bad eatin'," Junior said.

The conversation continued in this fashion for most of the meal until Mathis Senior looked at me and said, "Reckon you and me got to have a talk."

I nodded.

There was a long period of silence, an uncomfortable stillness for awhile.

Mathis Senior wiped his face with a napkin. "Junior, you best take that pretty girl out dancin' tonight, or I might just ask her."

"There's a dance over at Cooley's tonight," Jenny said.

Junior agreed as if he had no choice at that point. Mrs. Watson started clearing the table, and Jenny began to help.

I stood and took the dishes from her. "I'll help your mother. You go get ready." She resisted at first, but I was soon helping Mrs. Watson with the dishes. Watson and Mathis Senior left the room for awhile and returned when Mrs. Watson was removing the table cloth. Watson set a round container of poker chips on the table, and Mathis Senior, a bottle of whiskey. Mrs. Watson instructed me to sit down, and she placed three glasses and a bowl of pretzels on the table. She then left the room.

The setting sun cast an orange hue on the yellow walls briefly until Mr. Watson turned on the overhead light. Mathis Senior picked up the cards and began to shuffle. Watson asked me how many chips I wanted, and I gave him fifty dollars.

"Reckon we'll start out easy on the boy. Five card natural. Dollar ante." Senior started dealing the cards which slid quickly across the table. He picked up his cards and started to shuffle them around. "So, Steiner said you stopped by askin' 'bout Francis."

"Yes."

"Guess you ain't gonna let this go. Your bet."

"I'm in for another dollar." They both threw in a chip. I asked for three cards. Senior slid the cards off the top of the deck with his thumb only using his left hand. Watson and Senior each drew two.

"There was a lot goin' on back then. The coloreds was gettin' outta control. Had to set up a separate school for the white children. Coloreds couldn't afford their own for a spell. Well, folks was real mad I guess is what I'm sayin'. Bet's to you."

I tossed in another dollar. They both folded. I placed my cards with only a pair of fives on the table face down.

Senior handed me the cards. "You won the deal."

I started to shuffle. Junior and Jenny came into the kitchen both sporting cowboy boots, jeans, western-embroidered shirts, country-style ties and cowboy hats. They were both quite animated, Jenny pulling on him to go.

"You watch these old buzzards, James. Might be better off just givin' your money to me to hold for ya, or comin' dancin' with us," Junior said.

Mathis Senior looked at his son. "Reckon I won't be home tonight. You know how Momma Watson don't like me to drive too late." He winked.

Jenny pulled Junior out the screen door. "Thanks for helpin' with the strawberries, James."

Mathis Senior pulled out a cigar and handed it to Watson. He offered one to me, and I declined. "Wish that boy just go on and marry that girl. He's different 'round her. Just acts like a grumpy old man when she ain't 'round."

"Like you," Watson said.

"I'm happy out fishin'. That fool, Steiner. Bet he made you watch soccer with him, just sittin' there in a chair waitin' to die."

"He's a good man," Watson said.

Senior lit his cigar. "Yep. 'Cept he talks 'bout things shouldn' otta."

I continued to shuffle the cards and was growing very impatient, but I knew that they were going to explain this to me their way.

"Where were we?" Senior asked.

"That girl got raped," said Watson.

"Yep. You gonna deal sometime tonight?"

"Same game." I started dealing. The gentle hum of the tree frogs wafted in through the screen door.

"Like I said, folks was real mad." He puffed out some smoke that rose and hung around the overhead light. "White girl got herself raped and killed by a colored boy. Boy's momma turned him in 'bout a few months before your Daddy was killed."

"Two dollars," Watson bet.

Senior tossed in two chips. I matched.

Watson wanted three cards this time. "Damn shame that old gal havin' to turn in her boy like that."

"Felt sorry for her." Senior asked for two.

"Dealer takes two. So what does this have to do with my father?"

"Well, we got there and saw your father's and brother's bodies all chopped up some kinda gruesome. Never seen nothin' like it. Figured only some kinda lunatic do somenthin' like that. We found the ax just up the hill leanin' next to Francis' shack, blood all over it."

"Two more dollars." Watson sipped his whiskey.

"I'm in." Senior tossed in a couple of chips.

"Dealer folds."

"Three nines." Watson placed his cards on the table.

"Little straight." Senior collected the chips.

"Not as little as them fish." Watson dipped his unlit cigar into his whiskey and put it in his mouth. "It

made sense. Francis was always walkin' 'round the
campus carryin' that ax, mumblin' to the trees or
somethin'."

Senior started to shuffle. "Told me was squirrels."

I downed the rest of my whiskey and reached for
the bottle. Watson slid it to me. He took off his glasses
and wiped them with a handkerchief.

Senior set the cards down and continued. "It was
done. We had the weapon, the killer, and your momma
said she saw him do it."

I felt unusually warm and clammy. I filled my
glass. "But?"

Senior picked up the cards again. "Steiner."

"Boy, you're breakin' out in a sweat now. Go get
you some cool water from the spigot there." Watson put
his glasses back on. "Heard a joke other day." I drank
down some cold water. As I walked back to the table, the
tree frogs seemed to be inside my head again. "Two boys
is drivin' down the road in a convertible, top down and
all, drinkin' Bud bottles. They come up to a police check
point for drinkin'. So one tells the other to peel off the
label of the bottle and stick it to his forehead. So they pull
up, both with Bud stickers on their heads and the officer
says, 'Um, you boys been drinkin'?'

'No sir, we're on the patch.'" Watson started
laughing. "How 'bout that." Senior let out a full belly
laugh. I laughed along, and the tree frogs seemed further
away. I sat back down.

"Seven card stud," said Senior, and he began
dealing. "Two down, five up."
We all tossed in a chip. "Jack bets." I tossed in a chip.
They matched. Senior continued dealing. "So Steiner
comes to me after we done locked up Francis and says he
saw you carrying the bloody ax back up to Francis'
shack."

"I did?"

142

"Now you gotta understand a few things. Like I said, folks was real mad, and they was goin' to hang Francis no matter what. Jack still bets." I tossed in another chip. They matched. "Son, you look a bit pale right now. You need a break?"

"No...no. Where's Mrs. Watson?"

Watsons' Ace won the bet. He tossed in a chip. "Oh she's readin' that Romance crap, likes them books by that woman, what's her name, Steel. Bunch of bull 'bout true love and such."

"Knights in shinin' armor," said Senior. "You know her?"

I threw in a chip. "No. I couldn't afford to rent a closet from her."

Watson continued his rant. "No such thing. You meet somebody, get along and take care of each other. If and you're lucky, make a baby or two and nothin' bad happens. That's it."

Watson finally won a hand with two pair, and he handed the whiskey to Senior.

Senior handed the cards to Watson. "After Steiner come to see me, I talked with your momma. She told me what really happened."

"And?" I was clenching my fist.

"Said your brother's death was kinda accidental. You and your daddy was fightin' 'bout something, and Steve just got in the way somehow. Your momma got all wild and stabbed him."

"She..."

"She had you help her take the bodies out to the pasture near Francis' shack and make it look like Francis done killed 'em."

"Why...What were we fighting about?"

"Reckon was 'bout smokin' weed. All you kids was doin' it back then. Seventies, what a God awful mess.

But I never seen a stoner get rowdy like a man can't hold
his liquor. Most men can't at times, even Watson here."

"Hey," Watson said.

"Just that one time with Peggy, back when you
had hair." Mathis puffed on his cigar.

Watson nodded his head. "Reckon that's what
done happened. Your daddy was a good fella, played
poker with us, wasn't all snobby like them other
professors. Their feathers get all ruffled you don't call 'em
doctor."

"Five card, two's wild." Watson started to deal.

I searched Senior's hardened and wrinkled face
for more. "Something is missing."

"Yep. My glass is empty." He reached for the
bottle. "Thing of it was. We had already tried Francis,
and done sentenced him to death. Felt real bad 'bout it,
but somethin' saved us all. Turns out, Francis had a brain
tumor and all sorts of other cancers. County physician's
gotta look at folks on the death row. Silly thing. 'Bout to
die and he gets his first lookin' after."

"Your bet," Watson said.

Senior picked up his cards and tossed in two
chips. "You was a mess. Didn't remember nothin'.
Figured that was best. Couldn't testify to nothin'."

I tossed in two chips without looking at my cards.
"What about Francis?"

"Well--"

"I'm in," said Watson.

"Two for me." Mathis slid two cards toward
Watson. "I pulled some strings to delay the execution.
Doc said he had six months at best. So, I figured we
would take care of him 'til he died, lived better than he
done in that old shack. Fed 'im good. Took 'im out fishin'
every Friday for a spell. He liked fishin'." Senior seemed
tired suddenly. "That whiskey runnin' right through me."
He stood and walked toward the bathroom.

Watson pushed the bowel of pretzels toward me.
"It ate 'im up somethin' awful. He liked Francis."

I finished my drink. "So I helped kill them."

"No, son. You done what your momma told you
to do. That's all. Wasn't none of it your fault." He poured
some more whiskey in my glass.

I ate a few pretzels and chased them with some
whiskey. "What happened to my mother?"

"She set ya up in a boardin' school, and she
disappeared, vanished."

Mathis walked back in. "She thought it best for ya
to move on, not remember." He sat down and picked up
his cards.

"How many?" Watson asked.

I picked my cards up. "Three."

Senior won the hand again.

While he was shuffling, Mrs. Watson came into
the kitchen. "Now you boys ain't eatin' enough for all that
drinkin'." Very quickly, she placed a bowl of
strawberries, some rolls and strips of salted pork on the
table. "No ring 'round the moon tonight, so we gonna
have a nice day for getting' up the crops tomorrow."

"You finish that book yet, Ma?" Watson asked.

"No. I'm fixin' to get ready for bed. Lots to do
tomorrow." She picked up a strawberry and took a bite.
"That Jenny knows how to grow 'em."

Senior started to deal. "That was a mighty fine
meal, Nan."

Mrs. Watson stepped back to the table. "Now
don't keep this fine worker up all night. Hear he's good in
the field." She cupped her hand under my chin. "Now
don't bet your car tonight, sonny. You'll be stuck here
with us for a spell." She said goodnight and left.

"What're we playin'?" Watson asked.

"Five card natural," Senior said.

I focused my attention more on the whiskey and the delicious strawberries, and Senior proceeded to take a few hundred from me. The whiskey had numbed me almost to the point of not being able to stand. I wished them both a good night and stumbled up the stairs to my room.

"Hey sleepy head, time to get up." Jenny was standing over me. "Didn't turn the fan on. Must a been quite a game last night."

"Ice," was all I could say. She left the room. The chirping of the birds and the cawing of the crows sounded as if they were using loud speakers. I sat up. My legs and back were sore. Jenny returned with a large pitcher of ice water and a glass. I poured the water and ice into the wash basin and stuck my face in it.

Jenny handed me a towel when I pulled my face out. "Daddy just growled at me, and Senior cussed me. How much you lose?"

"Couple hundred." I sat on the bed.

"Got off easy then. Momma's keepin' breakfast hot for ya." She left.

I picked at the eggs and sausage but drank almost all the orange juice they had. Afterward, I went outside, and Mathis and Jenny were carrying large baskets of green beans to the pantry. Watson was perched on a rusty, red tractor with an empty trailer connected to the back. He had on a straw hat, and when I walked over to him, he placed a corncob pipe in his mouth.

"Think I'd make a good character for one of your books?" he asked.

"You are definitely a character."

While we gathered up the corn, Watson moved the tractor along, and Jenny, Mathis and I carried the ears over to it. The reality that I participated in the deaths of my father and brother along with the realization that the

dreams were my subconscious trying to tell me
something dripped through my mind as frequently and
randomly as the sweat dripping into, and burning my eyes
and the cuts on my arms from the corn leaves.

After we had filled the trailer, Watson drove it up
toward the house, his silhouette against the blue sky, with
the breeze teasing the strands of straw in his hat. It
seemed like a snapshot of times past, a picture of the
simple joy of the harvest.

At the house, the pickers, Jenny, Mathis and I,
went to the water pump while Mrs. Watson inspected the
load.

Mathis took an already soggy handkerchief out
and mopped his forehead. His blond hair was matted
down.

Jenny filled a large bucket full of cold, well water
and threw it on him and ran down toward the barn
laughing. Mathis took off after her. "James, you fill up
that there bucket." Jenny managed to out run him for
awhile, running in circles on the lawn. Then she hid in the
corn, popped out chastising Mathis and then ducked back
into the large green stalks. I pumped the handle to fill the
bucket and watched the rows of corn waving about as
Mathis pushed them aside, seeking his revenge. Her
giggling and laughter must have given her away, because
Mathis soon bound up the hill with Jenny over his
shoulder, lightly spanking her ass, part of which was
exposed due to the length of her shorts.

Mathis set her down on the grass in front of me.
"Tickle monster." Jenny was laughing. "Get that bucket
ready, James." I picked it up. "Now." He let go of her,
and I drenched her.

"Oh, now you's in trouble." She stood up and
promptly tackled me. "There's more than one tickle
monster 'round here." Her wet, red hair, fallen from the
pony tail, covered my face while she proceeded to find

every spot on my belly that made me laugh. I tried to resist at first, but it felt good to just laugh. Suddenly, she let go and stood. A large splash of cold water quelled my laugh and transferred it to Mathis who was standing over me with a now empty bucket. Jenny was laughing.

"Grab her," I said to Mathis. He did. I stood and tickled the hell out of her. We were all laughing. We finally all collapsed next to the water pump with exhaustion and occasional giggles.

"Is the corn the last thing for today?" I asked.

"That's it." Jenny said. "Momma'll decide what's for cannin' and what's for chickens."

"We'll sell some too." Mathis said.

"Your father said that there's only one more row to do." I wiped the wet hair away from my face.

"Sounds right." Mathis stood.

"Mr. Watson and I will take care of it. You two go have some fun for awhile." I knew that given how aroused I was from wrestling with Jenny in her scanty, drenched clothes, Mathis must certainly have been.

"You sure?" Mathis asked.

"Go." I said. "Before I fill up this bucket again."

Jenny stood and gave me a peck on the cheek. She turned around toward Mathis. "Wanna go down to the creek?"

He waved his hand for her to lead the way. "Reckon we already wet."

They headed down the hill, tickling each other in some kind of dance or ritual that struck me as both beautiful and honest. I wondered if I was meddling in their affairs somehow, if my perception of how much they cared for each other was my own projection, a vicarious adventure to ignore my inability to understand myself.

Watson had to actually get off the tractor and help me gather the last ears of corn. He didn't seem to mind that much and offered a few jokes including how one must watch out for crayfish when naked in the creek.

We parked the tractor and corn in the barn. The chickens seemed upset about that. "Ain't seen Mathis Senior since breakfast." He pushed down the brake.

"Probably out spending my money." I stepped off the trailer.

"You got off easy, boy. Went fishin'. Should be back by now."

I helped him close the barn doors, and we walked up to the house. Mrs. Watson handed me a glass of cold ice tea. "Seen Senior?" Watson asked.

"No." She handed a glass of ice tea to her husband.

Jenny and Mathis came through the door and into the kitchen, still giggling.

"Where's Pa?" Mathis said.

Watson shrugged. I waved my hands.

Mathis sat at the table in the same chair where I had lost a few hundred dollars and learned about my past, or at least a version of it. Jenny sat down and handed him an ice tea. "I know where he is," said Mathis. He stood up.

"I'll go with you," I said.

"Me too," said Jenny.

Mrs. Watson stepped away from the stove. "No, sugar, let them be. You need to help me with supper. Besides, you done had your fun already."

I followed Mathis out to his squad car. "Looks like it needs a bath."

"Just get in."

We drove down the back roads until they turned into mud. I was completely lost and yet recognized

everything. We pulled up behind Senior's truck. Mathis
stepped out. "Remember this spot?"

"I don't know."

"You came here with me and Steve one time,
fishin'."

We walked down a muddy path to a lake. The
cattails had released their seed. Little wisps of white fur
floated about in the gentle breeze. They became thicker,
stuck to our hair, and the smell of the lake started to
invade my nostrils, a dampness, something evolving
through the natural course of death.

"There he is." Mathis pointed. Under a large oak
sat Senior, his broad hat all but covering his face, his
fishing pole resting on his knee. We walked up to him.
"Pa, it's getting' late. Time for supper."

"Ain't caught nothin'." He looked at me. "You
boys bring any whiskey?" He held up an empty bottle.

"No, Pa. It's time for supper now."

Senior picked up his pole and started to reel it in.
"Ain't caught supper yet. There's another pole there."
Mathis put the bate on the hook and handed the pole to
me. I cast it into the lake, the red and white bobber
bouncing briefly on the calm, green water. "Francis liked
fishin' here. Spent more time watchin' the squirrels then
his bobber." He sat up and cast his line out into the lake,
not far from my bobber. "Called them chipmunks little
squirrels. Cute little rascals."

I handed the pole to Mathis, who sat down next to
this father. I stepped toward the lake, and the cattail seeds
floated about over the lake, some destined to drown,
others to float along and live. They were like giant snow
flakes falling into a warm breeze, floating and melting, all
without any control over their destiny. I sat down next to
Mathis on the huge root extending from the tree under
which Senior had chosen to sit and get drunk.

Mathis gave a light tug to his line to wiggle the
bait. Senior just stared at the falling flakes of cattail seed.
I didn't know what to say. "Francis liked fishin' here?"
"Died right where I'm sittin'." Senior said. "We
talked 'bout lots of stuff. He had a rough time of it.
Reckon the cattails will be here next year. Caught more
fish with Francis here seems like."
        "Pa, it's time for supper."
        "Gonna marry that pretty girl or keep dingin'
'round?"
        Mathis handed the pole to me. I started to reel in
the line.
        "Ain't that simple, Pa."
        "Sure it is--"
        "You two are great together," I said.
        "Now the both of ya." He stood. "I don't need this
kinda pressure."
        "You ain't gonna find a better woman in these
parts." Senior stood up and finished reeling in his line.
        I realized something that seemed, at least at that
moment, incredibly profound. "Are you afraid of being
hurt, that she might leave you?"
        "What if she up and dies? Then what?" He stood.
"Momma did, then Steve."
        "If you don't ask, I just might," I said.
        He punched the hell out of me, dropped me in the
mud. "Pussy writers from up north. What do know about
life, real life, nothin' that's what." He started pacing along
the bank. "Reckon you'll write some kinda poetry for 'er."
        I sat up and rubbed my jaw. "I have read a lot of
poetry and written some, but the most beautiful poetry
that I have ever witnessed might well be you and Jenny
when you're together."
        Mathis kept pacing. "I can't afford the damn ring.
That's the problem. She deserves somethin' special."

I started wiping the mud off my shirt. "Hell, your father took a few hundred from me last night."

Mathis stopped pacing. He walked over and held out his hand and pulled me up. "Sorry."

"No sweat. I like it when I can feel every part of the left side of my face in such an acute fashion." Even though it was painful, I feigned a smile.

Senior handed the poles to his son. "Boy, if you like her, I'll help you with that silly ring business. Never understood that. She gets a ring, and the groom gets what?"

We walked up the path with no fish and leftover bait. Mathis apologized again for hitting me. I said that I probably deserved it, and that he owed me a drink. We decided that Senior was drunk, so I drove his pickup with Mathis following behind. He directed me down the muddy roads.

"Nice thing you done there," Senior said.

"What?" I asked. The truck rattled along the road through bushy trees that seemed to object to our being there at all.

"Took that punch like that."

"I didn't have much of a choice really." I wasn't used to driving a column shift and ground back into second gear.

"Sure you did. Could a kept your mouth shut."

"That wouldn't have been much fun now would it?" I checked the rearview mirror and saw Mathis behind us.

"Turn here." We were now on macadam. "Guess not. He took his momma's death and then Steve's death mighty hard. Used to be the happiest, carefree boy, and after that, he just got way too serious 'bout things." He pointed. "Pull over here." I pulled up to a little store. Senior stepped out. Mathis parked behind us. After a few minutes, Senior returned with a string of fish.

"Looks like we caught a few today now."
I waved Mathis ahead of us to lead.

At the farm, Mrs. Watson fussed over the bruise
on my jaw. We had a nice meal, and Senior asked me to
point out which fish I had caught. I played along and
picked the smallest one in the pile. Senior seemed small,
weary. I wondered if my stirring up the past had opened
wounds that would have been better left closed. Jenny
and Mathis joked about some city boy helping out in the
fields. Jenny insisted on knowing why Mathis hit me. I
told her that I had just said something stupid about
fishing. I could tell she knew better, but she let it drop.

After dinner, I excused myself and went to bed,
this time turning on the fan before the mattress greeted
my worn body. The next thing I knew, Jenny was waking
me for breakfast.

Despite my stiff jaw, I cleaned off the plate very
quickly. They all objected, but I insisted on leaving. I
used the excuse that Oliver might be starving, which of
course was not too much of an exaggeration.

Mathis walked me to my car. "You come on back
now. We'll find you a nice girl here."

"Is your father okay?"

"He'll be all right. Reckon this had to happen at
some point. It's done now."

"You know, if you need help with the ring--"

We stopped at my car. "Daddy said he's gonna
give me all his Civil War stuff, and I can just go ahead
and sell it. You know rifles and pistols. Gotta pistol that
still shoots."

"I might know a man who would be interested. I'll
give him your number. His name is Stone."

Jenny came bounding down the hill, displaying a
glorious reason for the abolition of bras. "Wait." She
almost fell into us trying to stop. "Here." She handed me

a couple of bags. "That's the rule. Ya work in the harvest, ya get some of it, strawberries, melons and some corn."

I placed the bags into the backseat of the car. I looked at Mathis. He nodded. I gave Jenny a hug and a light kiss on the cheek. "Thank you for everything, and tell Mrs. Watson that those French chefs can't compete with her cooking."

Mathis held out his hand. "We'll tell her." I shook his hand.

"Come on back down for Thanksgivin'," Jenny said.

I gave them my best John Wayne voice. "Well Missy, I'm gonna get these strawberries up north." I looked at Mathis. "Pilgrim, you circle the wagons 'til I get back, and watch out for giant squirrels." That gained a rise of laughter, and I started the car and drove down the driveway. They were waving as I reached the main road, and I honked the horn.

Thick as a Brick

During the drive home, I felt an emptiness, an emptiness that I thought might have come from living in such a diverse world where I had no family, no grounding of any kind. I had felt grounded at the Watsons, if only for a brief time. It confused me since I had spent most of my life running away from Picketsville, away from what at the time had seemed like a lesser existence in a small pond. I had been running from my past as well. Yet I didn't really seem to belong in the city, or anywhere.

As the houses started to become more numerous along the road, I realized that I had grossly misjudged the Mathis' and the Watsons. They had protected me, but I then started to question what they had told me. I wanted to believe their story, and there didn't really seem like any reason to dispute their version of events regarding my involvement in the deaths of my father and little brother. It seemed all too convenient somehow, let me off the hook to a certain extent. But one thing did appear to be absolute. I had participated in their deaths. My dreams had been telling me this since I had gone back there to research the school closings that had occurred long before I had met Francis the Ax Man.

The annoyingly slow combines and produce trucks were replaced by eighteen-wheel trucks and expensive cars with drivers who seemed concerned about arriving somewhere forty-seven seconds sooner by driving like idiots. I wondered if I could possibly salvage something from all the madness. I wanted to see Mathis and Jenny get married and thought about how fun it would be to take Robin and Cynthia to meet them. I imagined how much Cynthia would like picking strawberries and tickle fights.

Oliver greeted me at the garage door with all the usual fanfare, including his tail stuck straight up and wiggling. He was almost out of water, and I of course immediately updated his food. I put the bags that Jenny had given me into the refrigerator, and sat down on the couch with the lemonade that I had bought along the road earlier. I turned on the news to find out what silly "breaking news" the cable companies thought deserved my attention. It was mostly the same garbage. Oliver finished crunching on his food and walked into the living room and lay down on the floor, his back to me. He let out a sigh to express how hurt he felt about my absence.

I watched the news and truly wondered if our society had completely lost even a whisper of sanity. All the news channels were carrying live coverage of a girl who may or may not have been related to the third cousin of another girl who was allegedly raped by someone who the first girl, now holding a press conference, didn't know at all. They had a full panel of guests to analyze nothing. No one knew anything, including the breaking news girl. This consumed about a half hour until I lay down and fell asleep on the couch.

Francis tips his hat. "Nice day fer fishin'." I cast in my line. "Them little squirrels is cute." He points at the chipmunks. They scurry away over the tree root. "Francis knows how to catch fish." My bobber is still. "First Francis gots to be real quiet. Then Francis just watch them squirrels and keep away from them nasty flies." The water is pink now, and I can't find my bobber. "Sherf come fishin' with Francis before. He nice."

"Is he coming today?"

"Francis be here when he does. He ain't got long now. Sherf be here soon, cause Francis ain't caught no fish since he stop comin'. Just fishin' and waitin' now."

There's a tug on my pole. I reel it. I see pink ripples. The chipmunks run by.

"Cute rascals. Give it a tug."
I pull and fall. The hook is in Sandy's mouth.
I awoke in a sweat and quickly sat up letting out a scream. Oliver jumped a couple of feet in the air and stood with his back arched and his fur prickled up as if he had stuck his tongue into an electrical socket. I sat for awhile staring at the muted TV and then noticed that I had a voice mail. It was a rather upset Stone. I called him back immediately. He said that he had tried to call me at the Motel 3, and they said I was gone.

"I was just about to put out a bulletin," he said.

"I'm sorry. I ended up staying with some friends. It won't happen again."

"Well, the reason I called was to tell you to stay there."

"What?"

"Just stay away from Mark. You may hear from Detective Green soon." There was some clatter in the background. "I have to go." He hung up.

I placed the phone back into its cradle. "Well, Oliver, I think you might like the country." I went into the kitchen and pulled some strawberries out of the bag. Jenny must have put a few pounds in it. They were bitter sweet, almost ripe, perfect.

While I was cleaning the kitchen and Oliver was intermittently swatting at my heels, there came a frantic knocking at the door. I opened it thinking it might be this Green fellow. It was Mark. His usual calm façade did not stand before me, but rather a sweaty, drunken man who had clearly been up too long on his product. "Jamie's dead," he said. I started to open my mouth, but nothing came out. "Dead. You have to help me. I got to get rid of the body."

"I can't…"

"She knows you killed your wife. Had to." His
speech was so slurred that it was almost not discernable
at all. "Can't find her here, not now."

"I… are you sure?"

"We can dump her in the lake." He pulled me out
of the house and virtually dragged me into his. Cindy was
sitting on the couch next to a limp Jamie who was
slouched to her left onto the arm rest. Cindy snorted a
line off the table.

I walked over to Jamie and felt her neck.

"Dead." Cindy snorted another line, a large one.

I looked at Mark. "I'll take care of this."

"Hey, man, I owe you." I picked up Jamie and
walked out the door.

I took Jamie into the house and then down into the
garage and placed her in the passenger seat of my car.
She still had a weak pulse. I drove like a lunatic until I
arrived at Shady Grove Hospital. I didn't bother with the
emergency waiting room and parked in front of the
ambulance entrance and then walked through the
automatic doors with Jamie in my arms. The security
guard hassled me at first, but he soon called over a
doctor. I told him that it was probably a cocaine
overdose. They placed her on a green gurney, and off
they went. All I recall hearing was the term, STAT.

I walked into the waiting room where there sat
many very impatient customers. The waiting room was
aptly named for its efficiency, or its lack of it. I went to
the pay phone and called Stone and left a message for
him explaining what had happened. Afterward, I went to
the admitting window and gave them my information and
shared what little I knew about Jamie. I was told to have a
seat. After I sat for awhile, I went outside and paced the
brick walk and watched the sky start to fill with clouds. A
thin fellow walked by wearing a red shirt and the
volunteer patch. I wondered if he could help Jamie like

the volunteer who had helped me the last time I was there.

I went back inside and walked up to the admitting window to find out what was going on. Apart from being obese and quite rude, the admissions clerk had the nerve to offer some condescending remarks about drugs and questioned how I could be involved with a girl half my age.

"Well first of all, I'm trying to save her life. What are you doing you functionary, Miss Piggy of a bitch?"

"I'll not tolerate that kind of rude behavior." She stood and placed her hands on her hips that wouldn't fit into any reasonably sized chair.

"Nor will I." I placed my hands on my thin hips. "I want to talk to your supervisor…now."

"Security." She waved to the guard.

"That won't be necessary." The voice came from behind me. I turned and there stood a tall fellow, sharply dress in an olive-colored suit, and his yellow shirt along with his vibrant brown and yellow tie seemed to make his black face almost glow. He showed his badge to the guard and then to me. "I already spoke with the supervisor. Let's take a walk."

"Who's going to pay for this?" Miss Piggy said.

I turned around. "Should've have been a bit nicer to me, don't you think?" Green's large hand pulled me away. We walked over to the concession area, and he bought us both a soda. We walked outside. An ambulance pulled up, and the white coats ushered out a body in a frantic fashion.

"Do you know who she was? he asked.

"We had this little fling, nothing really. Who are you anyway?"

"I'm with vice. Stone called me." He drank down some of his soda.

I started to take a sip of mine, but stopped. "What do you mean...was?"

"She's dead."

"What do you..."

He stopped me from walking and looked at me with his large, dark eyes. "She didn't make it. She had no wallet, no ID, nothing, a ghost."

I sat down on a nearby bench. "That's just what I need, another ghost."

Green went on to explain that he was the detective who was looking into Mark and that the cocaine I had given to Stone was indeed lethal in certain cases. He suggested getting out of town for awhile and emphasized that I should stay away from Mark.

He tossed his empty soda can into the nearby trashcan. "We may need you to testify."

I thought about Jamie's body lying on a green gurney with the sheet over her young face. "Whatever you need." I stood and started to walk toward my car.

Green handed his card to me. "There's was nothing you could have done about this."

When I arrived at my car, I noticed that I still had the empty soda can in my hand. There were no trashcans, so I just crushed it and set it on the passenger-side floorboard. Despite the time of day and the fact that I knew the sun was still overhead, it was almost pitch black from the clouds that had been blown up the coast by the hurricane. As I slowly drove home, I heard myself laughing. "Killing your wife is okay, just don't litter." My thoughts then turned to Jamie, how she really didn't deserve what had happened to her and how I had been complicit in her demise.

The wind started to blow harder, and my car swayed back and forth in the road like a boat on a choppy ocean. I stopped and picked up a six pack and a tuna sandwich, hoping that the latter of the two would be my first choice when I arrived home. The street lamps in my neighborhood were out, and my garage door opener didn't work. I parked in the driveway, secured the car windows and fought the wind to get out. I heard a banging and followed the sound around the side of the house. The wind was pushing the fence gate back and forth such that it appeared to be beating itself against the house. I braced the gate against the house with a few bricks.

"Psst." I started to walk toward the back door.

"Psst." Just above me, a murky figure was crouched down, huddling against the rails of Mark's deck.

"Mark?"

"Shhh. Come up to your deck," he whispered.

I walked under my deck and entered through the back door. The lights did not work either. I stumbled around through my office, cussed out whatever I stubbed toe on and went upstairs. There I realized how difficult it was to find a flashlight in the dark, particularly if you didn't know where it was. After I found it, I walked out on the deck.

"Turn that off, Man." I did. "Get down."

I squatted. "What--"

"Is it done?"

"She's gone." We were talking through the deck rails like two kids planning a water balloon attack.

"They're watching. I know they're watching."

A strong gust of wind almost knocked me over. "Who?"

"Not safe...It's done?"

"Yes." One of the white, plastic chairs skid across the deck. Then the wind knocked it over. It clattered against the house.

"Okay. Just be cool."

He was gone. I picked up the chair and sat in it. Soon, large pellets of rain smacked against me. I stripped off my clothes and piled them in the chair and stood in

the dark being bombarded by the wind and the rain. I
knew it wouldn't cleanse me, but it still felt good. I gave
in to my own helplessness. I couldn't control the storm or
Mark or even myself. I had no control over when my
electricity would return. It seemed that all I could do was
embrace it somehow, accept it all, like the rain drops that
through no fault of their own were being hurled toward
the Earth. The storm let up a bit, and I walked inside and
dried off.

I lit a scented candle and sat watching its flame
flicker. The smell reminded me of Sandy. She had an
affection for scented candles. They had not really done
much for me until now. The scent was sweet, vanilla
perhaps. It reminded me of some of our romantic
moments, and I could see her sitting down at the dining
room table and hear her complement my cooking before
she took a bite. Then I realized that it was in fact Susan
seated across from me at the table. She began fiddling
with Cynthia's presents.

"Those are not for you," I said.

"Nice wrapping job."

"I'm going to bed." I blew out the candle.

"Sweet dreams."

There was nothing sweet about my dreams. The
bodies kept piling up, over and over again--my father and
brother, Sandy, Susan, Jamie. Francis the Ax Man just
smiled under his tree and gave his fishing line a little tug.

I awoke feeling completely exhausted. The Lion
was sleeping at the foot of the bed, and Oliver was
hungry. He raced me down the stairs and into the kitchen
where Susan was completely naked and modeling
Sandy's jewelry. She didn't say a word, just kept arriving
in different parts of the house wearing a different
necklace or a different pair of earrings. I told her that she
could at least help me with the laundry as long as she was

teasing me. She ignored me, and I decided to return the favor by ignoring her modeling efforts.

Later that afternoon, I answered the phone. It was Karen, Sandy's sister. She asked if she could stop by in two days since that worked for her in terms of her schedule. I agreed and gave her directions. I also offered to put her up for the night, but she said that she would be staying with a friend. I felt a bit relieved by her response since I was not really very suitable to be a host at that point, particularly for a grieving sister of a woman I may have murdered. I couldn't remember what day of the week it was and soon discovered that I had no calendar for that year.

I went up to Sandy's office and shuffled through the mess on her desk looking for a calendar. There were bras and papers, a photo of us together in a canoe, jewelry in the oddest places. I had never understood how she could have been so adamant about cleaning the rest of the house while her office, her space, was such a mess.

I started to pick up and organize Sandy's things for her sister. Oliver came in and offered his usual help...comic relief and distraction. I tried to determine which clothes were dirty and wondered if I should wash them. Then, I started to wonder what to do with her lingerie and under garments that I had bought for her. I cycled between rage and despair as I placed them into a separate pile, all the while wondering if I should just get rid of them or maybe just ship them to Kevin Brown. Apparently she had worn them for him more than for me, the person who had paid for them. Susan came in to help as well. She thought that modeling Sandy's things would be useful for me. This only amplified the increasing pain of discarding Sandy.

I looked at Susan. "I killed her?"

"You know the truth." She plucked a pair of earrings off.

"I'm about as far from the truth as I could possibly be."

"Well, talk to your buddy, the Lion. Seems like you like him the best."

"Why do you taunt me so?"

She danced a little jig, her firm breasts barely moving. "Something to do."

"Well, put some damn clothes on…your clothes, not hers." I left the room.

Oliver followed me down the stairs, raced me rather. It was one of his self-appointed duties, to reach the bottom or top before I did. I wondered if I could be happy with such simple achievements, a clear goal, nothing complicated…kill, eat, get laid, just like the Lion had said. I pulled out the bag of strawberries, and while I ate a few, thought about how much fun picking them had been, how I had slept so soundly.

The next day, I readied myself to spar with Dr. Fowler. I put on my armor, a blue, pinstriped suit, red tie and matching silk braces. I polished my cordovan-colored dress shoes and told Susan to look after Oliver while I was gone. I packed up some strawberries, and after finding the garage empty, no car, I went out the front door and was relieved to see her in the driveway.

During the drive to Rockville, I wondered what to tell Fowler, what information I should reveal to her, how much I could trust her. I also wondered what information I could even call trustworthy. In the parking lot, I checked my armor, straightened my tie and smoothed my hair.

Inside, I wasn't sure if the receptionist noticed that I had remembered her name. She really didn't seem to care and waved me to have a seat. I chose to pace around the empty waiting room, hoping to see Robin.

Dr. Fowler walked into the room. "Mr. Douglas. I'm glad you came." She waved me to follow her to her office. It seemed almost the same. The tan leather furniture was just as I had left it, and her desk was neat to a point that invited me to turn some file or pen such that it was not perfectly aligned with the edge of the desk. "Please have a seat, Mr. Douglas."

I chose the same chair and sat down. "Something seems different in here."

She sat down, crossed her legs and pulled her black, pleated skirt down to cover the tops of her knees. She checked her fuchsia-colored blouse and shifted it such that the buttons were correctly aligned. "What do you think is different, Mr. Douglas."

"Please call me James." I looked around. "I don't know."

She picked up a file. "The last time we spoke, you were having trouble with the loss of your wife. How are you feeling now?"

"Oh. I brought you some strawberries." I stood and handed her the plastic container. She smiled. "That's the first time I've seen you smile, a genuine smile." I sat down wondering what she would look like with her blond hair released from her ponytail.

She set the file and notepad on the desk. "Should we have some now?"

"Why not."

She pulled a couple of napkins out of her desk and handed me one and then reached over the container. I took out a couple of the strawberries.

She ate one. "These are quite good."

"Picked these myself."

"I didn't notice your southern accent the last time you were here." She dabbed the napkin against her lips.

"I was in my hometown, down south…picking strawberries and playing poker. I suppose the accent comes back if you let it." I ate another strawberry. "Yep, found out I was involved with the deaths of my little brother and my father. You know, that missing year in my file."

She put down the strawberries. "How were you involved?"

"Stole an ax from Francis the Ax Man and chopped them up after my mother killed them, well maybe only my father. I may have helped to kill little Stevie. They told me it was an accident."

"Who told you?" Her words came out almost in a stutter.

"The girls thought my southern accent was real cute when I moved up here. Now my accent has been flattened out by this area, all the different dialects and languages. Shame really." I stood, stepped to her desk and pulled a couple more strawberries out.

"James, we need to stay focused."

I looked at her. "That's what's different. You're wearing glasses."

"Please sit down, James."

I sat. "But that's not even really the good part. I probably killed my wife, but I don't know, stories, nightmares. So, you like the strawberries?"

"Yes, thank you. Go on, calmly please."

"I'm worried about Robin." I loosened my tie.

She turned the page of her pad and kept writing. "Is that why you came here today?"

"Yes…I don't know." I started rubbing my knees. "I think Cynthia was molested."

"Do you think you molested her?"

I stood up. "No, damn it. Mister Walrus did."

"James, please calm down now." She was inching her hand over to a button on the desk, a security button perhaps.

I sat. "I'm sorry."

"Take a deep breath now."

I did. "You know, I didn't mean for any of it to happen. I think it's the Lion's fault, but he's my friend."

"Take a deep breath now." I did. Her face was completely pale, and strands of her hair had fallen on her neck and ears. "I don't know where to begin here."

"May I have another strawberry, please?" I asked. She reached over the container. "Thanks. Look, Cynthia was probably molested, and I frankly wonder if Robin wasn't as well. They need help."

"Dr. Weiner is going through a difficult time right now, and she and Cynthia along with Cynthia's mother are getting help."

"Will you tell her what I said?"

"That's all I can share with you, James." She set down her notepad and pen and leaned forward. "There's a program at Chestnut Lodge that might be able to help you with all of this."

"A program?"

"It's voluntary. You check in and work through things for awhile."

"So you're just going to pass me off like Robin did…like my mother did." I stood, tightened up my tie, and walked toward the door.

"Our time isn't up, James. We have a lot of work to do."

I opened her office door. "Sorry I ate so many of the strawberries, Kim." I closed the door behind me before she could say anything.

The receptionist tried to stop me. "Dr. Fowler says that I should schedule another appointment for you."

"Have nice day, Betty."

On the way home, I picked up some boxes, and as I carried them in, Oliver tried his escape through the garage door. I didn't bother to fuss at him, just scooted

him back into the house from the garage and told him that
we had some work to do. I took off my suit and put on
some shorts and a white tee shirt and proceeded to pack
Sandy's clothes. Oliver jumped into each box after I had
finished taping it together. I felt remorse, and yet an odd
calm, like Francis sitting at the lake, just fishing. He no
longer had his ax, simply a fishing pole and a small tin of
bait. Susan was of course upset that she would soon not
be able to torment me by wearing Sandy's things. I
wondered if that wasn't my primary motive to get rid of
her things, or if it was my attempt to find some form of
closure. It pained me to do it, but I took Sandy's lingerie
and put it into trash bags. When I had boxed all the things
in her office that I could, I went downstairs and fed
Oliver. I then glanced around the living room at the
various vases and crystal figures that she had collected
over the years and thought that I should pack them as
well, but I decided to simply go to sleep next to the Lion.

The next morning, I readied the house for Karen's
visit. I had never met Sandy's sister before and wondered
how things would go. I made sure to have a least one
clean bathroom for her to use and mused at my long
standing joke that a woman might accept rat shit in the
living room, but the bathroom had to be clean.
The dishwasher was still running, pans clinking,
when the doorbell rang. I opened it, and there stood a
plumper, blond version of Sandy.
"Please come in, Karen."
She walked up to the living room. "How did you
know it was me?"
"You have the same brown eyes as your sister." I
pointed to the couch. "Please have a seat. Can I get you
something?"
"A restroom would be nice." I pointed to it.
"Thank you."

When she came out, I handed her a bottle of
water. "I'm sorry," I said. She sat on Sandy's couch. I sat
in my chair. Susan took a seat on the stairs and played
with her dirty-blond hair. "That's her couch."

She was wearing what Sandy would have worn:
knee-high, washed-denim shorts and a loose shirt that
partially covered her rear. She took a long drink of water.
"My brother wanted to come with me." She screwed the
cap back onto the bottle. "I thought that he might be too
angry still, so he doesn't know that I'm here."

"I packed her things up as best I could for you."

"Where's Oliver?"

I looked around. "He's probably hiding. He's not
very good with guests."

"You are taking care of him." She crossed her
legs.

"Yes. He's my buddy. Are you ready?"

"Sure." She had the same accent as her sister,
New Jersey.

We walked up the stairs, Susan leading the way
with a frown, and we went to Sandy's room. "I did the
best I could with this. Everything in this room is
hers...yours now if you want it." She looked around the
room and then at me. Her eyes were watery, distanced
and confused. I caressed her shoulder. "Take as long as
you need." I walked out the door and brushed the tear off
my cheek.

I walked back down the stairs and thought that I
should wrap up the crystal and things that Sandy's mother
had given us. I taped a box together and with some
newspaper began wrapping the crystal. I decided to wrap
the flower vase that I had given Sandy along with a dozen
roses for our first anniversary. It seemed to take forever.
Each moment of that night flowed slowly through my
mind while I gently folded each corner of the paper
around it. I knelt and placed it into the box with the other

pieces. I walked over to the bookshelf and picked up a ceramic vase. Something rattled inside. I tilted it over, and a silver, pearl-shaped earring clattered onto the coffee table. I picked it up.

"James can you give me some help?"

"I'll be right up." I tucked the earring behind some books and went up stairs.

She was standing there next to a couple of boxes that she had taped shut. "I don't think I should take her clothes." She handed a picture to me. "I think you should keep this one of you two."

It was the shot of us in a canoe. I opened my mouth, but no sound came out. Karen wrapped her arms around me and gave me a hug.

"She was crazy about you." She stepped back. "Even after you started your writing."

I nodded and picked up one of the boxes that she had taped up and carried it downstairs. She followed with another. I pointed to the box of crystal on the couch and went back up to get the last. We packed the boxes into her car in the driveway.

She closed the trunk. "I should probably go."

I nodded.

"Are you going to be okay?"

I grabbed her hand. "I'm sorry." I opened the car door for her. She squeezed my hand and then got in. She backed out of the driveway and waved. I waved back and then walked up the stairs and back inside. I sat in my chair. Then I picked up the phone book. I began looking for the number to the Salvation Army. I knew that I could not endure another scene like that. I needed it to be over. I scheduled a time for them to come pick up Sandy's couch and her clothes. That was only a temporary distraction from the earring which I had hidden behind the books earlier, the same earring that Mark described, the earring that I had taken when I had killed her.

There were bright lights outside, flashing lights, red and blue coming through the transom window above the foyer. I quickly rose and looked out through the blinds. Several police cruisers were parked in front of the house. Running out the back door was my first thought. It perished slowly to the weight of my weariness with all the pain, death and confusion. I simply unlocked the front door and cracked it open. I sat in my chair waiting for them to come take me. The phone rang.

"This is James."

"James, it's Robin." She sounded upset.

"I miss you. Are you okay?"

"Listen. I know you had a difficult session with Dr. Fowler yesterday."

"We ate some strawberries."

"My sister is in the same program that she suggested to you. I'll take you there if you want."

"I may have some more immediate problems right now." There was a knock at the door. "I have to go. I...I have some presents for Cynthia." I hung up. "Come in." I sat with my hands in clear view, resting on the arms of the chair.

A uniformed officer walked up the stairs, his gray hat in his hand. "I saw that the door was open, and thought I should check. Is everything okay here?" He looked around and leaned back to check the kitchen. He had his hand on his holstered gun.

"I don't know. What's going on out there?"

"We just arrested your neighbor. Had a good tip."

"Oh?"

"Sure you're okay?"

"I'll be fine. Thank you for checking, officer."

He stepped back down into the foyer. "You should keep this locked."

I followed him to the door and watched another officer protect the top of Mark's head while placing him

171

into the back of one of the white cruisers. The blue and
red lights stopped, and the cruisers drove away. I closed
and locked the door. I dialed *69 to get Robin's number,
and afterward sat in my chair wondering if I should use it,
whether or not I should get her further involved in my
problems. Cynthia's presents convinced me to reject my
reticence to call Robin despite the fact that her husband
might answer. Robin answered and agreed to meet with
me.

We met at the same deli in Rockville where we
had shared our first dinner together. She was sitting at a
corner table in the back.

"Chicken tenderloin?" I asked.

She looked up. Her eyes were bloodshot, her hair
unwashed. She feigned a smile.

"I'm glad you came." She motioned for me to
have a seat.

I started to lean over to kiss her, but she turned
away. I sat down across the table from her. "I'm sorry
about earlier. Things have been a bit goofy lately."

"I think this program might be able to help you."
She didn't look up.

"You said that your sister is there?"

"Yes."

"Please look at me."

She looked up. Her eyes looked like brown, half
moons. Her upper eyelids seemed to strain to remain even
partially open. "I'm sorry. I...after Kim, Dr. Fowler,
called me, I was worried about you."

The same waitress with her red hair tied back in a
ponytail arrived at the table.

"I'm afraid you missed lunch. Here are the dinner menus."
She turned.

"We'll split an ice cream sundae," I said.

Robin's frown soften a bit. "High school?"

"Sugar."

"You need to go into this program."

I took a sip of my ice water. "What's bothering you, honey?"

"They took Cynthia away from me. She's with my father now."

"Why...Mister Walrus?"

She started to stand. Her hands shook. "She's with Mister Walrus now." What little color there was left in her face drained away, and she sat and bent her head toward the table. "You have your own problems. You don't need mine too."

The waitress delivered two spoons and a sundae. She looked at me, nodded and handed me the bill. I nodded back. I stared at the sundae and at the top of Robin's head wondering how I might possibly offer any advice or inspiration that would be useful.

I grabbed her hand and placed a spoon in her palm. "I suppose I'll find out if I'm still lactose intolerant. Of course Kim might say that I'm generally intolerant." She raised her head.

I raised my spoon as if I were about to engage in a fencing match. "Only this moment exists. Two people who care about each other fighting over who gets the most walnuts." I grabbed the bottom of the sundae and started to slowly slide it toward my side of the table.

"Hey." She grabbed my wrist. "I haven't had a sundae in years."

We both started to enjoy the whip cream and vanilla ice cream, dipping it into the fudge. She scooped out a walnut. "Nice psychology there. This doesn't let you off the hook though. I want you to go to that program. Please."

"What do I get?"

She licked her spoon. "What do you want?"

"I want you and Cynthia in my life." I found another walnut in the fudge.

173

"It's complicated right now."

"I don't care. I understand that it's a package deal." She said nothing, and we sat silent for awhile. I pulled out the cash for the bill. "I bought some coloring books for her."

Robin looked away. "She likes Chef James."

"Oliver likes her. I've never seen him so affectionate with a child before." I pushed the bill and the money toward the edge of the table.

"She's with my father now. I had taken her away from him as soon as I found out she was there the first time." Her voice was filled with angst and frustration. "I know what he does."

The waitress came to the table and collected the money. I told her to keep the extra. "How do we get her out of there?"

She stood up. "This is not your problem."

I stood and grabbed her shoulder. She looked up at me. I looked into her eyes. She started to blink after a bit. I just stared, a cold stare I imagine. "If anybody dings with you or Cynthia, they will deal with what is behind these eyes."

We walked out into the balmy, August evening, the sun almost done with its day. "That's what I'm afraid of."

I turned toward her. "What?"

"What's behind your eyes." She kissed me on the cheek and walked away. I stood and watched her walk to her car. Even her steps seemed tired, almost misplaced as if her feet wanted to walk in a different direction.

After getting into my car, I turned around and looked out the back window to make sure that she was safe. I then noticed that I had not removed my travel bag from the car after my visit with the Watsons. Although I didn't really want to, I started driving home. Robin's voice echoed between my ears. Her pleas for me to reform through therapy were genuine, and the pain and concern in her voice seemed to settle in my gut which felt empty and lost. An internal debate began with the part thinking that if J truly loved Robin and Cynthia, I would give Chestnut Lodge a try.

Gone Fishing

It was indeed fortunate that Robin had already given me the sales pitch and the incentive to check in to chestnut lodge, because the receptionist offered the demeanor of disgruntled waitress at an all-night diner. The only difference seemed to be that her uniform included a white hat. While I filled out the various forms, I confirmed that my attendance there was completely voluntary…several times. I finished the paperwork and handed it to her along with my credit card.

"This is vol—"

"Yes, Mr. Douglas. You can leave whenever you want."

"And—"

"I'll call Dr. Weiner for you."

"Oliver—"

"I'll tell her to feed your cat." She waved her arm

"His name is Oliver." I stood up and started turning toward the door.

"Sir." A large coffee-colored hand firmly gripped my shoulder. "This way. I'll get you settled in." He picked up my bag. He was a large fellow with short, curly hair with a few wisps of gray that intermittently sparkled beneath the yellow lights that were protected by brass-colored cages. We turned a corner, and then stopped. He reached into a room and turned on the light. Susan was sitting on the bed. I started to pull away. "Now, the bathroom is across the hall, and if you need anything, my name is Al." He set my bag on the bed and closed the door behind him.

"How did you find me here?"

"I told you, James. We're connected."

"You hardly ever leave the house."

She rocked back and forth on the mattress between the iron-metal bedposts. "Yes, well it's a lot nicer than this dump." She stood. "Bars on the window?"
      I looked at the black bars. "Those are for my safety."
      "Are they here to keep people out, or you in?"
      "Leave me alone. Go see what the Lion is doing."
I started unpacking my bag.
      "Sleeping. He's no fun."
      "Yes. Sleep sounds good."
      "You're just doing this for Robin."
      I turned out the light and groped over to the bed, took off my shoes and stared up into the darkness until my eyelids finally closed and Susan's taunting no longer mattered.

      I awoke feeling refreshed despite the fact that I could not have slept for very long. I sat up and rubbed the sleepy dirt from my eyes. My dreams were of lost memories of catching crayfish in the creeks with my little brother and later of Sandy when we married, how happy she was. I did of course dream of her dead body again, but somehow, there was some form of cathartic release from all of it, a necessary cleansing of my mind. Susan's absence encouraged my hope even more. I felt like writing, and I was quite hungry. I was doing the right thing for Robin and Cynthia.
      The green corridor led to a dining hall that had an adjacent room which appeared to be a game room of some sort. It was all white except for the mauve-colored tables and chairs. Apparently I was a bit late since there was no line to get breakfast. I slid my tray along and asked for everything—bacon, sausage, eggs, pancakes, and since they were out of waffles, I ended with a large glass of orange juice on my tray. I found an empty table and sat. I couldn't get the food inside me fast enough. I

went back and picked up another orange juice and came back to my table where a small, bald-headed man was sitting. I sat down opposite him. He had light-green eyes with slits for pupils.

"I'm Chester," he said. He reached out his chubby, little hand.

I shook it. "James."

He looked over both his shoulders. "Don't eat the eggs."

"What?"

"Eggs are bad." He looked around again. Then he bit into a piece of melon. "Don't eat the eggs." He stood and left.

I returned my tray and started to wander around a bit. In what seemed to be the game room, I saw a couple of chess sets, and then one with a fellow sitting at one, just staring. I had not played chess in years and thought this might be fun, but I didn't wish to interrupt. I stood and watched him for awhile. His face was narrow and topped with thinning, yellow hair that seemed to not wish to be brushed. His eyes, partially hidden beneath black-framed glasses, stared at the chess game. His thin fingers rested on the table next to the board. He didn't move. I started toward the table.

"Mr. Douglas."

I turned around. "Hi Al."

He hand me some pills in a cup and a cup of water. "Dr. Fowler prescribed these for you. She'll be by to check on you." He stood there and watched me take the pills. "She said to tell you that your cat is fine."

"His name is Oliver." I handed back the empty cups. He turned and walked away. I looked back at the chess guy, and he was still sitting there. I felt an urge to get my notebooks and write about these interesting people. I hurried down the hall to my room. Thankfully, Susan was still gone, but the color of the room,

institutional green, struck me as completely hideous. I
fumbled through my bag and found only some three-by-
five cards. I scribbled until both sides were full of mostly
random thoughts. I went to search for Al to get some
paper. Loud screaming drew me around a corner. Beyond
it, Al and a few other large men in white smocks were
subduing a woman. She was screaming, "No...No."
       "Calm down now," Al said. "We need to get you
back on your meds."
       Her limbs flailed about in the air while they
carried her away.
       I could taste my breakfast in the back of my throat
and felt feverish. I managed to walk back to my room and
lay down.

       During the next few days, I took the meds every
morning and evening like they said I was supposed to, but
I often threw up. I stared at the pad that Dr. Fowler had
given me when she told me that it takes awhile to adjust
to the medication. I couldn't write at all. I didn't dream at
all.
       It may have been a week or so, and despite the
fact that I was tired of seeing the yellow puke on my
jeans everyday, I was eating my breakfast hoping that it
would stay down this time. Chester sat down at my table.
"Eggs are bad. Pepper too." He rubbed his hand over his
bald head.
       "How long have you been here?"
       "I'm billing hours."
       "Hours?"
       "The lawsuit. It's time for a walk, then TV time."
       I stood and picked up the tray.
       "Leave the tray," he said.
       I set it down, and we walked down the green hall.
I stopped, doubled over and the yellow came out all over
the green smock that they had given me. I leaned against

the wall, sweat streaking my face and neck. Chester was gone. I doubled over again. I thought that I would soon see my toes coming out of my mouth. The white coats came with a fresh smock and cleaned me up.

"You're doing good, Mr. Douglas." It was Al.

I started to lunge at Al. Chester grabbed me. "It's nice outside. James right?"

"Yeah, I guess."

I had a clean smock and the same familiar raw taste in my mouth. Chester walked me down the hall and outside and sat me on a wooden bench. I bent over for a moment, trying to remove that all-too-familiar feeling of having just been punched in the stomach with a sledge hammer.

When I sat up, Al handed me a bottle of water. "You're doing fine."

I took a sip, gargled and spit it out on to the browning grass.

"You can't tell anyone about the lawsuit," Chester said.

A woman in a green shirt ran by us. The curls of her brown hair floated above her.

Chester sat next to me on the bench. "Christine. Doesn't like eggs now, 'cause I told her." His round face seemed pale, floating next to me.

"That's Christine?"

"Pretty when she wants to be, if you know what I mean." His hand was on my shoulder.

I looked up at the waving branches of the oak trees above. "The leaves will turn soon. How is your lawsuit going?"

He stood. "I'm filing a motion tomorrow." He shook his tiny fist. "I'll get the bastards."

"Go Chester." I stood.

"That's right."

I watched Christine and realized that she was the same girl that I had seen being carried down the hallway, Robin's sister, Cynthia's mother. Christine ran up with a stick. "A flower for you." She winked. Her eyes reminded me of Robin.

"Thank you." I took the stick that she handed me and waved it in the air. It whistled. "You have a lovely daughter. She likes Oliver."

Her smile fell away. "What did you do to her?" She grabbed my shirt.

"We had fun, tuna melts, a bath, played with Oliver."

She slapped me. "So you call it Mister Oliver."

"Oliver is my little buddy." My cheek hurt.

She shook me. "That's what Daddy says. That's what Daddy says." She ran away.

Chester's face was in front of mine. His gray eyebrows furrowed. "We may need to investigate the law on this."

"Yes, I may need a good attorney soon."

"You don't have to take the meds."

We went back inside, and Chester said that he needed to go work on his briefs. I thought it was time to play chess. I sat down opposite the fellow who had been sitting in front of the same game in play since I had arrived there. He didn't stir. I examined the board. I moved my knight out to threaten his pawn.

He moved it back. "That won't work." He just stared ahead as if that would be a normal response. I tried moving the bishop. Same response. This went on until I stood and knocked over my king. "Yep. That's your only move." He stood and left.

I went back to my room and decided that the meds had turned my mind into a day-old bowl of oatmeal, and my clothes into targets for half-digested eggs. I wasn't dreaming either, and despite the rude nature of my dreams, I longed for them now. I knew that they came because they were necessary, and that repressing them expelled me into an existence void of creativity of any kind. I wanted to write. I decided to check out, but I soon realized that I was incapable of operating a car. After all, I had trouble navigating the bathroom to take a shower.

Over the next few days, I faked taking the meds, and like Chester said, I didn't eat the eggs. Al must have figured out that I wasn't taking the meds and called Dr. Fowler.

There was a light knock on the open door to my room. Dr. Fowler walked in wearing her blond hair down. It fell nicely on the top of her black pantsuit and white blouse. "How are you doing, James?"

I stood and shook her outstretched hand. "Green is a bad color for me." I pulled on the sleeve of my smock.

She sat in the little wooden chair. "I understand that you want to leave now."

"I'm leaving." I turned and looked out the barred window. Christine was talking to a tree, an oak.

"Do you think that is wise?"

"Yes. You know...I really don't much care for yellow for some reason now."

"You volunteered to be here."

"I'll volunteer somewhere else."

"James, we have other therapies. We'll find something for you."

I turned around and removed my green smock. "The only therapy I need right now is to start writing again. A blow job and a stiff drink wouldn't hurt either." I pulled a tee shirt out of my bag. "Not necessarily in that particular order."

She leaned back and crossed her arms across her breasts. "James, there's no need to be crude."

"I'm sorry if my writing offends you." I shoved
my notebook into my bag and picked it up. I walked out
the door and down the hall.
She followed, her black heels clicking on the
yellow floor. "James, we should talk some more about
this."
I kept walking. "Your clock is out of line with the
edge of your desk."
She grabbed my arm. "Give it some more time."
I opened the door, scaring the birds into flight.
"The slows ticks of your clock? I don't think so."

The small, red leaves of the burning bushes
around my house were scattered everywhere, including
the steps up to my front door. Inside, the house seemed
unusually clean. It even smelled nice, warm somehow.
There was potpourri in a little dish on the oak, CD holder,
and I wondered if Sandy was home. I set down my bag
and sat in my chair next to a stack of phone messages and
unopened mail. I started to pick them up, but then I
realized that Oliver had not greeted me at the door.
After I searched the house, I read the messages.
Several were from Stone. A couple more were from
Mathis, and there was one with the number of Oliver's
vet. I immediately called it. They had Oliver. He was
sick.
I drove over there immediately. He was in a little
cage and looked about as miserable and frustrated as I
felt. His orange fur was matted. He seemed thin when the
girl with the long, black hair took him out of the cage. He
tried to scratch and bite her and then me when she
virtually threw him at me. I tucked him into the brown,
plastic carrying case that Sandy had bought. To say that I
was angry would be a gross understatement. She adjusted
her white smock over what might actually turn into
breasts someday.

"I'll get your bill." She walked away from the other caged animals.

"I'll speak with the vet. Now is convenient for me..." I wanted so much to add the word "bitch" to the end of that demand.

He was a short man with gray eyes and a comfortable tan. He advised me that Oliver's kidneys were acting up again. He spoke of my buddy as if he were just a thing. I bought some more of his special food and paid the bill. Then I took him home.

He immediately ran upstairs after I let him out of the carrier. I looked at the pills that I was supposed to shove down his throat twice a day. I understood why he had chosen to run. The pills were ridiculously huge, comparable to a human swallowing a golf ball. I somehow resisted my anger and didn't call the vet.

Instead, I went to the store and bought an eyedropper. My food buying relationship was apparently still in tact at the local grocery store, and the liquor store seemed content with my credit card.

Back at home, he didn't greet me at the door. I assumed that he needed some rest, maybe some dreams. I crushed up one of the pills in a bowl and set the eyedropper next to it. I poured a tall glass of whiskey and then sat in my chair trying to explain all this to Sandy.

"Who are you talking to?" Susan was sitting on Sandy's couch.

"Is the Lion still here?"

"He's sleeping for now."

"I need to get rid of that couch." I stood and plugged my guitar into the effects board and flipped on the mixer and CD player. I tuned her up, put in a custom disc that I had made and jammed along with some of my favorite southern tunes from the seventies. When that was done, I wiped the sweat off my face with my white tee shirt and inserted another disc which I had entitled

"Classic Rock." I was about halfway through a Stones' tune when I saw Robin sitting in my chair. I took off the headphones.

"You startled me."

"Sorry," she said. She looked the same. She seemed unkempt, and there was no light in her eyes at all.

I pulled the guitar strap over my head and set her down on her stand. "I missed you." I reached for her cheek.

She turned away. "You left the clinic."

"Yes." I walked into the kitchen and called Oliver by shaking his bag of dry food.

She followed. "Why?"

I kept shaking the bag. "The food sucks, and I hate the medicine. I can't write." I clicked my tongue, calling my buddy. "I stopped taking those drugs a few days ago."

"Let's sit down and talk...please." She straightened her green tee shirt and tucked it into her jeans. We went into the living room and sat on Sandy's couch, no Oliver

"I'm worried about you." She rubbed her bare, creamed-colored arms. Her head was bent toward the floor.

"The Lion will take care of things."

She looked up. Lines, a sadness had formed in her face, colorless and without hope. "You need to give the medicine more time."

I stood. "Time for what? Time for Cynthia to end up like your sister?" I started to walk back and forth from the foyer to the couch. "Not on my watch."

"James--"

"What are you going to diagnose me with now? Hell you don't even have a diagnosis that makes any damn sense."

"Rage." She pointed toward the stereo.

I stopped pacing. "What?"

"I saw so much rage while you were playing the guitar, the songs you chose, all rage." She straightened her back. "Your eyes were closed."

I resumed pacing. "Maybe I have Chronic Fatigue Syndrome. Then again, perhaps I have Oppositional Defiance Disorder. Or better yet, maybe I have Generalized Anxiety Disorder. How about that?"

"James, please." She waved me to sit down.

I widened my arms like a bird's. "How about Post Traumatic Stress Disorder?"

"Stop." She stood up.

"Used to be called Shell Shock...good, simple words...Of course we can just throw drugs at these problems. Maybe cocaine was the best therapy for me. Then again, I just might suffer from Generally Pissed Off Syndrome. Look that up in your APA guide." I walked out to the kitchen and shook Oliver's bag of food. "What are we going to do about Cynthia?" I walked back into the living room, and Robin was sitting on the floor, her back against Sandy's couch.

I knelt beside her. "We have to help Cynthia."

She pushed me back. "You don't know a damn thing about it." She stood up and walked toward the door.

I stood, grabbed her arm and turned her around. I pulled her close to me. "Your eyes were closed when we made love."

Her brown eyes looked into mine. "Let go." She pushed my chest.

"Rage."

She pulled away.

"You close your eyes when you make love. Aren't one's eyes also closed by rage?"

"James, you have some form of disassociative disorder." She sat down on the stairs next to Susan.

"Yes, let's by all means make this as complex as possible."

"James, calm down please."

I walked over to the stereo and pointed at my cherry-colored Fender, my ax. "She is my love...and my rage. It's all one thing."

"James--"

"And that's another thing. Why don't you call me honey or something. Hell, even a coke slut called me tiger." I looked at Susan. "She's dead now." Susan giggled.

"I'm sorry about Oliver." Robin started to stand.

"He didn't like it when I just called him the cat." I grabbed her and pushed her onto the couch. Her breasts bounced beneath her green tee shirt. I wanted to feel her nipples against my lips. "It's time you met the Lion."

She started to hit me. "Don't ever--"

"Your father raped you and your sister."

She turned her head away. "Stop."

"That's why she's at Chestnut, and you can't handle intercourse, only oral sex. But you have to be in control." I realized that I was shaking her and stopped.

She stopped hitting me and looked up, her eyes milky with tears. "Cynthia..."

"My point exactly." I let go of her.

After a moment, she sat up. "I'm going to take care of that bastard." Her voice was calm, slow and delightfully deliberate. Her eyes stared blankly at the muted TV.

"I'll take care of it." I reached behind the books and found Sandy's earring. I placed it on the table. "This is the souvenir that I took from my adulterous bitch of a wife...right after I killed her."

"What are you saying?"

"I'm saying that I killed her." I pointed at the earring. "There, I said it. Now since we both know that I'm a murderer, what are we going to do about Cynthia?"

Robin looked down at the wood floor. "It's the same pathology. It's always the same." She cupped her hands over her face.

I sat down in my chair. "I once dated this woman before I met my wife. She was well educated, a teacher of English lit. Funny thing about it, she always sounded like a parrot, just repeating what others had told her to think, no original thought. It came to a point where if I had heard the words 'Daddy says' one more time, I may have killed her too." I looked at Susan sitting on the steps. She adjusted her torn, turquoise-colored sweater, the ice sliding down her yellow hair. "Maybe I did. It's time for some original thought."

She looked up. "I don't...this is--"

"Looney Tunes?"

"I'm a trained professional, and I do not understand you."

"It's simple, honey. I'm a murderer. I live with a ghost of a woman that I probably raped and killed." I pointed toward the stairs. "She's sitting right there. And I live with the Lion, although he has been a bit sleepy of late." I stood and walked around behind her. "I'll wake him soon."

She looked at the stairs where she had just been sitting. "James, there's nothing there."

I rubbed her shoulders from behind her. "I'll take care of Mister Walrus."

She gabbed my hands. "And then what?"

"I have high friends in places."

She turned her head around. "You're not stable."

"Really? No shit." I started laughing. "Are you?"

I suppose it must have been contagious. She began to smile, a weak and timid smile. Still, it fed my

desire to right my misdeeds and pass along something to
someone else without any conditions. Perhaps I wanted
Cynthia's light to endure all this madness. None of this
insanity was her doing, and I was determined to spare her
the burden of the past. I asked Robin to wait. I then
searched for Oliver. We had played a game over the
years, sneaking up on each other, but we each had our
sanctuary. His was my walk-in closet. I had never
bothered him there.

He was curled up on an old ski jacket on the floor
in the back. What was once a white coat was now mostly
orange from his fur. He looked up at me with glazed eyes.
I had to give him his medicine. He didn't fight me until
we arrived downstairs, he in my arms. I filled the dropper
with water and the crushed medicine, tilted his head back
and made him swallow it. Afterward, I showed him that
his food and water had been replenished. When I let him
go, he immediately ran upstairs. I walked into the living
room. "Let's roll."

Robin stood up. "The cops…" She ran her fingers
through her hair. "Court…"

"Cynthia. Now let's go. Charlottesville, right?"
She nodded.

"Give me just a minute." I went upstairs and
asked Susan to look after Oliver while I was packing a
few clothes into a bag. The Lion stirred, winked at me
and then resumed his nap.

During the drive to Charlottesville, I cracked the
sunroof to let in the crisp, fall air. Robin sat and just
stared out the window for awhile. Then in a very
controlled and even voice she explained that after
Christine checked into Chestnut, Christine's husband had
dropped Cynthia off with her father, Mister Walrus.
Robin had discovered this and took Cynthia away from
him. She then took the poor girl home to an abusive

husband who hated children and was divorcing her.
Mister Walrus filed a petition with the courts, apparently
Cynthia's father had signed over custodial rights to him,
and the authorities came and took Cynthia. Robin's
pending divorce interfered with her being able to show a
stable home environment, and Cynthia was doomed to the
care of Mister Walrus.

"I'm sorry I got you involved in this." She rubbed
my knee.

"Just another day at the office." I pulled my hand
away from the gearshift and stroked the back of her hair
which felt as though it had not been washed in a few
days. I wondered if she thought of me as somewhat the
same thing that I thought of myself, a monster, a
necessary monster. I tried to think of witty or comical
things to say to lighten the journey, but my wit had fallen
prisoner to a focused rage. We road along in silence for
awhile. I could tell we were getting close when she
started to wring her hands in her lap. Robin told me
where to turn when we were near the horse farm.

We pulled into the driveway. I felt strangely
exhilarated. I finally possessed a purpose. The farm sat in
a hollow just behind a small knoll. The fences were
rustic, three boards running into each post. The absence
of barbed-wire suggested that the horses were well
trained, like the daughters of this man. I stopped the car
behind the knoll as Robin instructed.

"This is it," Robin said. She opened her door.

I grabbed her shoulder. "We need a plan."

"We are going to get my niece. That's the plan."
She stepped out of the car.

We crept along the dirt and gravel road toward the
house, my nostrils were filled with the fumes of manure
and the damp leaves around us. She moved along the path
ahead of me. A bright moon, not a Peach Moon, but a
glowing, giant pumpkin seemed to be perched upon the

dormant trees. I wondered what face it would reveal this night. I couldn't tell if it was smiling at me, or was casually enjoying the foolishness of our consciousness. There was a dim light coming from the house windows that offered a direction to our stalking. We reached the front porch.

Robin grabbed my arm. "If I'm not back--"

"This is my task. Stand near the door."

"I'm going around back. Give me a minute." She disappeared around the side of the ranch.

I waited a bit. Then I pulled up the brass knocker that was shaped like a horse and banged it several times against the door. I banged again. Nothing. The door was unlocked, and I went inside. The home was dimly lit with only one light coming from the back of the place. But I could see the horse trophies on all the tables and on the mantel over the fireplace, all dark oak or cherry perhaps, and ribbons hung from the dark cross beams of the ceiling. Beneath the mantle was a stone fireplace with a stack of wood ready for a match. I heard a click.

"You best clear on out a here." The voice was confident and gruff.

At first all I saw was the barrel of a shotgun peaking out around the base of the stairs. Then I finally met him. He didn't really look like a walrus. He was shorter than me, but his shotgun was far more than I had to offer to the confrontation. I was after all in the man's house.

"Where's Cynthia?" I asked.

"Who the hell are you?"

"I'm working for Detective Stone. I have a warrant to pick her up." I pointed to the three-by-five cards in my shirt pocket.

He clicked the hammer of the gun closed and lowered the barrel. "Let's see it."

Robin rushed him from behind, knocking the gun out of his hands and pushing him to the floor. "Where is she, you bastard?" She pushed the gun toward me. "Where?" The gun skid across the boards to just a step away from me.

"Honey," he said.

She kicked him. "Where, damn it?"

"Upstairs. Your room." It almost sounded like he was sending her to her room.

She kicked him in the head and ran up the stairs. I had no clue how to operate a shotgun, but I picked it up.

"I'm bleeding." He started to sit up.

"Good." I hit him in the chest with the butt of the shotgun. He curled up into a ball on the dark planks of the floor. He moaned.

"How's it feel to meet the Lion?" I could scarcely see him given the level of light. I could mostly hear Robin's footsteps thumping overhead, and then she came down the stairs. Cynthia was draped over Robin's shoulder, motionless. Robin handed her to me and took the shotgun. She cocked back the hammer.

"If you ever touch her again…no you deserve this." She pointed it at him. The huddled figure began to rise from the shadow cast by the staircase.

I reached for the gun. "Robin, not in front of Cynthia. Not now." Cynthia was limp against my shoulder. Her hands didn't reach up to help or hug.

Robin looked at Cynthia. "Sweety, I'm sorry."

"Robin, I'll take care of this. Take Cynthia and go to the car." She lowered the barrel of the gun. "Now." I grabbed the gun with my free hand. "Go."

She took Cynthia. "This isn't your fight."

"Go. I have nothing to lose."

She carried Cynthia out the door.

I looked at the foggy figure knelt in front of me. "So, Mister Walrus, where do you clean your guns?"

"Get out of my house."

I grabbed his ankle and dragged him into the dining room where there was more light. "Raped your own granddaughter." I stopped and lifted him onto a pine chair next to the table. "What the hell is the matter with you?"

"You don't understand." He bent over in the chair clutching his chest with both his pale hands. Blood dripped from his nose onto his blue, flannel shirt.

"What don't I understand? What?" I placed the barrel of the gun against his throat.

He looked up. His green eyes seemed almost contrite. "I have to. It's my job."

I could now see his pudgy, round face, sadly decorated with wrinkles and whiskers "One of your daughters is in an asylum. She thinks that tree branches are flowers."

He gently pushed the gun away from his throat. "You've been there haven't you?"

I pulled the gun away from his reach. "I met Christine."

"No. I can tell by your eyes that you know. You know about the hunt, the control." He groaned as he straightened up a bit. "Ever see two horses mating? It's not a discussion. No bullshit, just fucking, control, no cocktails after dinner and a movie and a blow off kiss. He says we're doing this. That's it."

I lowered the gun. "Like the Lion."

"Exactly." He coughed.

I sat in the adjacent chair and placed the gun on the table just beyond his reach. "You know, I had envisioned a gun-cleaning accident for you about now."

"What do you want?"

I leaned forward. "I want Robin to have full and complete custody of Cynthia."

"What's it to you?" He pulled the tail of his shirt out and dabbed the blood dripping from his nose.

I thought about his question, and I did not like the answers that seemed so eager to call themselves to my attention. I was particularly upset that they chose to arrive at that very moment, a moment which was previously replete with clarity and purpose, now a moment of self-loathing and confusion. I picked up the gun and walked to the end of the table. I sat down at the opposite end from him. The gun clicked against the table. I looked across the table and had the horrible thought that I was looking at myself in twenty years. "I love them." My hands started to shake.

"So do I." His voice was commanding. "You just want them for yourself now."

"I came here to kill you." I raised the gun.

"I saw your eyes. You're just like me, a predator...what did you call yourself...a lion?"

"Fuck you. Fuck you" I stood and cocked the hammer. "They're mine."

"Sure the gun is loaded?"

"Guess we'll find out." I walked around the table. His lack of physical aggression convinced me that I had a live round in the chamber.

He leaned back. "Go ahead. Be like me. Hell, I'd do it to have them all to myself."

The screaming faded into my ears like it was coming from an approaching train. His speech was incoherent as I suppose anyone having just had his right foot partially removed by a shotgun blast would be. I paced the floor during the screaming. I pushed him onto the floor. "I'm not like you." I kicked him in the face. "We are not the same."

"I'll get you," he mumbled.

"You should be more careful when you clean your rifles."

"You're like me."

I started toward the door and then turned back. "This is me in a good mood. Think about that, Mister Walrus."

"Fuck you and your family."

I pulled the door open. "That already happened." I wiped my prints off the gun with the drapes next to the door and dropped it. I turned around. "I'm allowing you to live for the moment. Tend to your horses and leave us alone."

The moonlight guided me back to my car where Robin sat with Cynthia nestled against her chest. Nothing was spoken. I could almost feel the pain radiating from them. I started my car and headed south. I cracked the sunroof to let in some fresh air. The only thing I heard was the whistling of the wind for quite some time. I pulled over at a roadside stop and touched Robin's arm. She stroked my arm and then my cheek. Her hand felt warm, needed. I stepped out of the car and called Mathis from a payphone. His office patched me through to him. I explained the situation and asked his advice. He said that he would call the Watsons and tell them to expect some guests.

I returned to the car with a some beer and pretzels and a couple of lemonades and candy bars. Cynthia and Robin did not seem interested in any of those things. We resumed our journey.

Finally Robin spoke. "Where are we going?"

"Some place safe, friends."

She pulled Cynthia tighter. I turned onto the road to Watson's place. "Did you...I heard the shot."

I down shifted and flipped on my high beams. "He's alive. He'll just have a bit of trouble walking."

"He's still alive?"

"He won't be able to drive a car for quite awhile either."

"He'll try to get her."
"We'll figure it out. We have some time."

Second Helping

I parked the car at the Watsons' place. A misty ring clung around the pumpkin, now almost directly overhead. I opened Robin's door. She stepped out with Cynthia still draped over her shoulder. I grabbed the beer and pretzels, and we walked up the path to the porch. Mrs. Watson stepped out to meet us.

"Well, ain't that a purty moon tonight."

"I'm sorry to trouble you--"

"No trouble. I was just fixin' some sandwiches for the boys." She waved her hand. "Y'all come on in. There's plenty."

We walked back to the kitchen. I pulled out a chair at the table for Robin. Then I handed the beer to Mrs. Watson. She grabbed my hand and patted it. Her black eyes were kind, stoic. I offered a smile. She put the beer in the refrigerator. Then she picked up a plate of cookies and set them on the table. "Now, who are your friends?"

Robin stretched out her hand and introduced herself. "I'm sorry to bother you."

Mrs. Watson placed her hands on her hips. "Now there're be no more fussin' 'bout that." She leaned over and touched Cynthia's arm. "And who's this sweety?"

Robin stroked Cynthia's bare legs that extended from her short, red skirt. "This is my niece, Cynthia." Cynthia looked catatonic.

"Well, she sure is a cute one." Mrs. Watson looked at me. "Got your room all ready, but y'all should eat somethin'."

"Maybe I should show them the room, and then we'll be back." I helped Robin up.

"Lot's of food here, ham, chicken. Made them cookies this mornin'." We started up the stairs. "I'll fetch you some fresh towels."

The room seemed like an oasis, humble and yet elegant in its simplicity. I had slept well there during my previous visit. I hoped the same for these two aching souls that both seemed pale and bereft of hope. Robin lay Cynthia down on the bed.

"You need to eat, Robin."

"Her legs are cold."

"I can bring up something?"

She bundled the white quilt around Cynthia. "I can't take her home." Her voice crackled. "He'll come get her...the courts." She sat down next to Cynthia and caressed her hair so lightly as if she were not even stroking Cynthia but rather her own painful memories, a replay of the abuse by her father that had occurred almost three decades before, comforting a ghost.

It seemed best to leave them alone. After all, I was, as Robin had said, unstable. "I'll check on you two in a bit." I left the door cracked open and walked slowly down the creaky stairs. In the kitchen, Mrs. Watson seemed to have a glow about her. Her face was pink, almost matching the rose-colored dress that had a small tear in the right sleeve.

She pointed at the kitchen table. "You sit now." I sat and stared at the iron mountings on the yellow walls. She opened the refrigerator and pulled out a side of ham, a wedge of cheese and a tomato. She placed them on the table in front me. Soon a loaf of bread arrived. She handed me a beer. "What do you want on your sandwich?"

"Thank you. The beer is fine for now." I twisted off the top.

She sat on the opposite side of the table. A strand of her gray hair fell against her cheek. "Mathis Junior said you was in trouble."

"I didn't mean to...I didn't know what else to do."

She waved her hand. "Its tradition. Heck, we done seen your daddy through those affairs your momma was havin', them ones Senior told you 'bout." She opened her beer.

I nodded as if I knew what she was talking about. She took a sip.

"Nice to have someone to talk to at night. Boys always out, seems like."

"Strange thing...what happened with my parents?"

"Oh, your daddy, he was a some kinna mess some nights. Come over here drinkin' with the boys." She started making a sandwich. "Senior had to drive him home. Mr. Watson drove his car back to the campus in the morning." She stood and pulled some plates out of the cupboard. "Tough thing for a boy to hear 'bout his momma." She bent over the table and sliced the sandwich in half. "Seems like yesterday." She pushed the plate with the sandwich toward me. "Yep, women's movement. Girls was all up in arms 'bout equality. Bunch a foolishness you ask me." She set another plate on the table and started to make another sandwich. "'Spect they just want to sleep 'round and have abortions." She waved the knife. "Maybe so they can just act stupid like men...no offense."

"None taken." I sipped my beer.

"Anyway, 'spect they took all that out on you sometimes, your folks. Wasn't your fault. You was a nice boy, still are."

"I don't know about that." I finished my beer and stood up. "May I help?" I felt dizzy and leaned on the table. "Can you look after them for a bit, please?"

Mrs. Watson grabbed my arm. She led me into the living room and sat me on the sofa. "You rest now. It'll be fine." I sat there staring at the dark walls, shadows wrestling with the fuzzy light from the hall.

A switch had been thrown. My thoughts rambled at first. Then a clarity that might only derive from madness, or perhaps madness from that clarity, began to reveal itself in what I perceived to be a waking state. The only emotions left in me were rage and guilt, each blaming the other for its presence. I could feel the waterfall between my ears growing louder and louder. I worried that Mister Walrus was right. Maybe I was just like him. I could see his eyes and hear the timbre of his voice as though it were part of the waterfall. "You're just like me."

"No I'm not damn it." I was standing now.

"James?"

"I killed an adulterous bitch. That's different. That's different."

"Have a sit now." Mathis had his hand on my shoulder. His eyes were a bit red, and the bitter-sweet smell of whiskey filled the air between us. He was out of uniform wearing simply jeans and a red and green, flannel shirt.

"I'm glad to see you." I started to leave the room. "We need--"

"Let's sit on the porch for a spell." He walked me out onto the porch. The air felt crisp and cool. The waterfall running through my body, through the Lion's luminous egg, calmed.

"'Come back for more of my wife's good cookin'?" Through the orange glow of the moonlight, I could see two figures sitting on the lounger. Mathis walked by and took the pint from Watson. He took a gulp. Then he handed it to the other figure there.

"Junior says you got some troubles?" It was Senior's voice.

"I..." All that occurred to me was how much of an understatement that was.

"Here, have a tug." A splinter of light off the bottle showed me where to grab. My eyes were slowly adjusting to the darkness. The whiskey tasted good, burned in a good way.

"Pumpkins be in soon," Watson said. He accepted the bottle from me.

Senior cleared his throat. "Hell, that means that ole Steiner gonna make me come visit him in that death trap and give out candy to them silly kids."

I leaned against a post. "Halloween. When the spirits of the underworld surface while life is being renewed."

"Don't know nothin' 'bout spirits. Just know he can't wait to see me in that hospital, thinkin' I'll have to be. Well, I ain't goin' like that, sittin' 'round waitin'."

"Pa you know plenty 'bout spirits." Junior started laughing. "Hell, you done cooked 'em up in your back yard for a spell."

Watson and Senior started laughing too. I guess I was smiling. My face felt lighter for a moment.

We passed the bottle around again, and I explained Robin's situation.

There was silence for awhile and another round of drinking. An owl lightly cooed, warning the night of its presence. It sounded so alone, almost remorseful that it would soon find and kill something to eat.

"Son, them Cutler boys still owe us a favor?"

"Reckon they do."

"Well?"

Mathis pushed his shoulder against the post and stepped away from it. "Yep. Shot 'im in the foot you say?"

"He'll probably press charges," I said.

"Don't worry none 'bout this Walrus fella now." He pulled me away from the post.

"I don't understand?"

"I know some folks up there owe us a favor. Let's get you a sammich."

"Reckon we gonna be kin soon," Senior said to Watson.

"'Bout time." I heard Watson say when Mathis and I stepped through the door.

In the hallway, Mathis stopped me. "Thanks for tellin' me 'bout that Stone fella. Bought three rifles and the pistol."

"That's great." We started walking again.

"Said he's 'bout to arrest a murderer."

"Yes...he is." We stepped into the kitchen.

Mrs. Watson was sitting at the table. She looked up from her game of solitaire. "They're fine, sonny, sleepin' now."

Jenny walked in. She seemed particularly radiant, but wearing a slight frown. "That poor girl." She rubbed my shoulder and smiled. "They's gonna be all right though. Be pickin' pumpkins soon." She gave Mathis a kiss on the cheek.

"I'm sorry...I didn't know what else to do." I picked up the bag of pretzels near Mrs. Watson's card game.

"Y'all be fine here for a spell," Mrs. Watson said. She started collecting the cards for a fresh game.

"I have to go back...I should check on them."

"Don't be silly. I made up another room for ya, just in case..." She looked at her mother.

"Mrs. Weiner says she don't want no men 'round her girl right now." Mrs. Watson started to shuffle the cards.

"That's probably best." Then I noticed the ring on Jenny's finger. I grabbed her hand. "That's beautiful." I smiled at Mathis. His face seemed a bit flush. I thought that it might just have been the booze.

"You comin' to the wedding?" Jenny asked.

"When?"

"Thinkin' May," Mathis looked down at his cowboy boots.

"Can't wait. I need to go now. I have some things to do." I pulled out my money clip and placed a few hundred on the table. "If they need anything, call me. I'll be in touch soon." Mathis and I walked down the hall and out onto the porch. I couldn't tell if Watson and Senior were still there.

"Wait." It was Jenny. We both turned. "Take some of these strawberry preserves with ya."

"Thank you."

"Maybe give one jar to that detective Rock, no Stone, yep." She pinched Mathis. "Thought I didn't know 'bout all that." She started giggling with a rhythm that reminded me of Cynthia's giggle when she played with Oliver, and given the darkness, it might have been her. I almost started back into the house to see her, but I thanked Jenny for her kind gift. The owl didn't sound far away when Mathis and I started back toward my car. The porch steps creaked, and my eyes slowly adjusted to the moonlight while we walked down the hill. I opened the car door. "Thank you for looking after them."

"Don't worry none 'bout it. They'll be fine. 'Sides, Jenny likes kids. 'Spect she'll show 'em how to carve one of them spooky smiles in a pumpkin."

"Well, that's a good thing since Jenny's pregnant."

He grabbed my shoulder. "What're you talkin' 'bout?"

I touched his throat just below his Adam's apple. "This part is filled in on her. It's full, not indented slightly."

"She ain't said nothin'."

I sat in the car. "You might want to move up that wedding date." I set the preserves on the passenger seat. "Thank you for your help, and congratulations."

"Don't worry none 'bout your girls."

I drove slow at first, watching the sides of the road for possums and deer. I almost turned around. Picking pumpkins seemed like a good idea. I thought about how cute Cynthia would look running around the patch, and Robin doting over her. The waterfall continued, and I could feel the shuttering. Sandy's face appeared on the yellow road signs. I knew that I needed to confess before I lost the nerve.

Oliver didn't greet me at the door, and I checked his food. It appeared that he had not touched it, but the water dish was empty. I found him upstairs. He was watching Susan do her hair. She said nothing. The Lion seemed comfortable on the bed, and I took Oliver downstairs and gave him his medicine. I let go of him, and he started for the stairs and then sat at the bottom. He looked back at me. I made a little bed for him on the loveseat with a few of my shirts and placed him on them. He watched TV with me for awhile until I drifted off.

I awoke with the image of Sandy's bug-infested face lingering from the nightmares.
The police station told me that Stone was on vacation. I picked up Sandy's earring and drove over to his house. Stone answered the door wearing his blue overalls and an orange shirt. His black hair was unkempt and looked like a poorly fitted toupee.

"Well, you must have received my messages," he said.

"We need to talk."

He showed me back to his study. "I'm glad you're here." He pointed at the wall of rifles. "Thanks for giving me Sheriff Mathis' number." He picked up a pistol. "There's a lot of history in these guns." He handed the pistol to me. "A man should know his history."

"Yes, but--"

"Can you put that up there?" He pointed at his display wall. "It's a bit high for me." I placed the pistol on the display rods above the other weapons and turned around. He motioned for me to have a seat next to the desk. It was bare except for a bottle of wood cleaner and a white rag.

He stepped back from the display. "That looks good there. I just need a sword now." He sat in his chair on the other side of the desk. "Did you stop by to congratulate me or to gloat?"

"I came to confess." I pulled the earring out of my shirt pocket and placed it on the table. "I killed Sandy. That's the earring that I took from her when I did it."

He picked it up. "So it did work."

"Yes it worked. I strangled her and took the earring as a souvenir."

"Where did this happen?"

"You already know where, the Shady Grove Metro stop. The lights were out…construction."

He placed the earring on the table. "What was she wearing?"

"It was a pink scarf, paisley with some other colors." Stone started playing hockey with the earring between his hands. "White stockings, blue skirt, white blouse." I looked down at my knees. "Lying slut…just like my mother."

The sound of the rolling earring stopped. "She was wearing a black pantsuit. Kevin Brown confessed a couple of days ago. That's why I left you messages to contact me."

I looked up. "What?"

"His plan almost worked. It was rather clever really. In fact, it might have worked except for Mark." He pulled an ashtray and a pack of cigarettes out of the desk drawer.

"I don't understand."

He offered me a cigarette. I pulled one out of the pack and set it on the desk. "His original plan was to plant the evidence, the earring, in your house when he came over to visit you. He did, but it was after we had already searched your place." He fumbled in his desk drawer. "Now this is the interesting part. Kevin was dealing coke through Mark, and Mark owed him a great deal of money. So Kevin enlisted Mark to set you up in order to pay off the debt." He pulled out a book of matches and set them on the desk. "Mark was to frame you with the murder of Jamie and drug possession. Kevin thought that by framing you for one murder, we would just go ahead and close the murder of your wife and blame it on you." He tapped the butt of the cigarette against his thumbnail. "Anyway, Mark realized that you were…how shall I put it…not exactly stable."

"I've heard that a lot lately."

"Kevin knew about your past adventures with drugs from your wife--"

"That bitch." I stared at the dark-wood walls, shiny from polish.

"Mark thought that if he got you high or drunk and then later told you that you had confessed, he would have some leverage over you, or perhaps induce you to confess like you did just now. It all backfired when you turned him in for dealing." He lit a match and offered me a light. I waved my hand. He lit his cigarette. "Detective

Green has Mark now. I really can't tell you more than that."

I just sat there for a moment watching the smoke drift toward the open window.

"You did a good thing."

"Are you sure'?"

"Mr. Brown pled to Murder Two with a sentencing recommendation from the D.A. for cooperating in the drug investigation. It's done."

"How long?"

"That depends on his cooperation." He stood. "He won't be practicing law anytime soon."

"Why did he kill her?" I looked at the guns.

"He won't say. I think that she was either leaving him to go back to you, or she was threatening to tell his wife for some reason. It's done, son."

"But..." I leaned my head down and started rubbing my eyes with my left hand... "the dreams..." I sat there staring at the dark wood floor trying to make sense out of all of it. I didn't know what to think about Susan. Even if I confessed to her death too, Stone would probably dismiss it as a confession from a deranged man.

"I know it's a lot take in." He starting limping around the desk. "We should have drink to celebrate." He opened a cabinet. "I have some single malt here somewhere."

"I really should go. I've been enough trouble."

"Stay. Have a drink." He placed the glasses on the desk and poured a shot in each. "This may be my last case." He slid a glass over to me.

"Thank you." I picked up the glass.

He raised his glass. "To my retirement."

I raised mine and we drank. "Retirement?"

He poured another shot into our glasses. "Well, it's not really official yet, but let's just say I was told that I should spend more time with my wife, take some time off. What the hell. Go out solving a major case…thanks to you." We raised our glasses and drank. "Mathis said that you resolved things there about your past."

"I appreciate your help with that."

He sat. "No big deal. A man should understand his past." He picked up the bottle with an expression that asked me if I wanted more.

I shook my head.

"I'm sorry about your wife. I suppose I'm being a bit callous now."

"No harm done. You know, your wife might like a bird cage during the winter."

"Now you sound like my daughter."

"I'll take that as a compliment." I stood. "I can show myself out." I started to leave the room.

"I'm sorry I was so hard on you."

I turned around. "She was in many ways a good woman."

He nodded. "Next time you talk with Sheriff Mathis, tell him I'm waiting for him to find that sword."

"Okay…Thanks again." I closed the door behind me.

I slowly walked to my car, stepping on the crunchy, brown leaves that lightly danced across the walkway in the crisp autumn breeze. I wondered about Sandy's and Susan's deaths. I felt both relieved and confused. During the drive to Stone's place earlier, I had been completely convinced of my guilt. I had also planned to later confess to killing Susan as a means of reducing my sentence through a plea bargain of some sort. In any case, I was determined not to seek an insanity defense. Death or jail seemed like a better option than turning into just another zombie at Chestnut Lodge, completely numbed through so-called medication.

I started up my car and began trying to sort through the dreams, but they were stored or catalogued in a random fashion with no sense of time or place, just fragments of metaphors and images with just enough lucid parts to offer some meaning to my waking existence. Yet, their meaning, if there was one, seemed to exist beyond my grasp, like a star that you can see out of the corner of your eye, but not when you look directly at it.

Stone's comments about Sandy's clothing forced me to cycle through the bits and pieces of those dreams that remained within my conscious reach. She was always dead and wearing the wrong clothing, at least not the clothing she was wearing when she died. It seemed that my dreams about Sandy were not repressed memories, but perhaps the projections of a guilty mind. Yet the dreams of Francis the Ax Man, while murky at times, did appear to be valid and indeed the slow surfacing of repressed memories. In those dreams, he was alive.

This left Susan.

At home, Oliver raised his head off the loveseat and offered a hoarse meow. Susan of course decided that she should hassle me. She was completely naked. "I'll follow you wherever you go. We're connected."

"Go to hell."

She waved her arms. "Here we are."

"What do you want from me?" I walked out into the kitchen.

She followed. "I'm just having fun. Are you having fun?" Her voice had the cadence of a nursery rhyme.

I pulled a can of soda out of the refrigerator. "Yeah, just a blast...a real hoot."

I walked back into the living room and sat down. "Even jail too. You'd follow me there?"

"Anywhere, my sweet." She played with her yellow hair.

I sipped my soda. "Even death?"

"Especially there." She sat next to Oliver and started filing her nails.

The Lion crept down the stairs and yawned, looked around and went back up to bed.

I finished the soda and turned on the stereo. I then picked up Oliver and placed him on a pillow on my lap, put the headphones on and listened to the wondrous beauty of Mozart, a beauty so intense that it always forced a constant stream of joy and pain from my eyes to drip down my cheeks.

Over the next few days, Susan continued her relentless harassment, but at least she was no longer part of my dream world, which had become relatively calm. I called Mathis, and he said that the girls were fine and that Robin would be in touch soon. He also added, "That Walrus fella ain't gonna bother nobody no more." I didn't ask him why. It seemed best not to know.

Oliver wasn't eating his food at all. So I went to the store and bought a whole chicken, potatoes and green beans for dinner. Despite his condition, needing special food, he always ate some turkey or chicken with us on special occasions. I thought it might get him to at least eat something.

Back at home, I put the bird in the oven. I then engaged in an argument with Susan about what color drapes to buy. This bled into discussions about throw rugs and towels, and then she finally complained about the real source of her anger, the potpourri that Robin had placed in the house while I was at Chestnut.

Every time I walked into the kitchen and opened the oven, Oliver stirred and poked his pink nose up in the air and let out a meek meow. "Almost done, buddy. Then we have some writing to do." I stroked his matted fur.

The phone rang. "This is James."

"Can we talk?" It was Robin.

"Of course. How—"

"I'll be right over." She hung up.

Susan scowled at me. "I'm your girl now, James. You might as well accept it."

"You know, by killing you, I must have done some man a great favor."

"Yes…you." She primped her hair.

"Go see what the Lion is doing." I nodded toward the stairs.

"You're not the boss of me."

"Robin is coming."

"Yes. Robin." She pointed her finger at me. "Did she ever tell you that she loved you too? Look at all you've done for her, that ungrateful bitch."

"Hey."

She walked up the stairs.

I straightened up the house and then set the table for dinner. While I was chopping the potatoes, I heard keys at the door. Robin walked in, and she looked much better. Her cheeks radiated a healthy pink, and her top eyelids seemed to no longer have bricks glued to them. She had cut her brown hair short, almost butch, and had lost a few pounds. I wiped my hands with the kitchen towel and walked over and hugged her.

I stepped back. "You feel good," I said.

She brushed my bangs off my forehead. "It's nice to see you too."

I looked toward the kitchen. "I'm making dinner. Are you hungry?"

"We need to talk," she said with authority.

I waved my hand for her to have a seat. She sat next to Oliver who curled over onto his back in his favorite, cute pose.

I sat in my chair. "How's Cynthia?"

"She's much better." She pulled her thigh-length, purple sweater up to the top of her blue jeans so that she could cross her legs. "Thank you for your help." She looked at me as if I were her patient and not her lover.

"I'm making some chicken, set the table—"

"When are you going back to the institution?"

I stood up. I could see Susan's feet on the stairs just below the dividing wall. I looked down at the floor and slowly walked over to the CD cabinet and closed it. "Not now, Robin," I said with my back to her.

"You need to go back." Her voice was quite stern. I turned around. "Why?"

"They can help you." She stopped scratching Oliver's neck.

"Help me do what?"

"Be normal. Have a normal life." She uncrossed her legs and leaned forward.

I turned around and walked into the dining room. "Like yours?" I started pruning the prayer plant on the dining room table. The Lion was sitting next to the table. He winked at me.

"I care about you. You can be better." Her voice wavered slightly.

"Then we can have a normal life?" I tucked my finger into the pot, and the soil felt dry. "Give me your sales pitch on a normal life."

"You need to go back into therapy. Chestnut would be best."

"Give me the pitch. What do I get?" I plucked a couple more dead leaves off the plant.

"Sanity, James."

I took a deep breath, tossed the dead leaves into the trashcan and walked back into the living room.

"Kill her, James," Susan said. She was sitting on the bottom step now.

"Shut up, Susan." I motioned for Susan to leave. "Robin...the correct answer is...us."

"Don't you understand that you are talking to things that don't exist?"

The Lion growled.

"Your sister talks to trees while she's on the medication. Do you have any idea what goes on in that place? Who are you to determine what does or does not exist? Now, what about us?"

She looked away. "Cynthia likes you. She asks about Chef James and Oliver."

"I thought we could take her to the Woodley Park Zoo…see the lions."

"If…"

I waited for a moment, but she didn't finish. "If what? If I am mentally and emotionally castrated?" I felt my voice rising and sat in my chair to calm down.

"Go James," chanted Susan.

I leaned forward, my elbows resting on my knees. "Is that the kind of man you want?"

Robin looked down at the floor. "Cynthia is unstable, and…you met my sister." The sadness and frustration in her voice was disturbing. "I have my hands full right now."

I could see her caressing Cynthia after our confrontation with Mister Walrus, the pain in her eyes. The vision was so disarming that I almost wanted to make her happy and go back into therapy. "Robin…" The Lion shook his head. I fanned the edges of my manuscript. " I came to you almost ten years ago to help me with cocaine addiction. You did, and I thank you. In fact my affection for you and Cynthia helped me resist some recent temptations in that regard. Now you're asking me to go on drugs, drugs which turn one's mind into mush and one's faculties into a helpless mess, a source of revenue." I stood up and picked up my VISA card bill. "Here, would you care to see what I paid in order to learn how to throw-up correctly and lose any sense of self-determination?" I paced the living room in a circle, my bare feet slapping against the wood floor. I stopped in front of her. "I'm going to create art, such as mine is, and I will not subject myself to this notion of labels and normality. Maybe the way I see the world is real." The Lion nestled his head against my leg.

She looked up. "Do you hear yourself?"

"In more ways than you can possibly imagine. You want simple solutions, yet you are more convoluted than a political speech. I am what I am. Accept it or don't. It certainly didn't seem to bother you when we were lovers or when we were at your father's house and you thought I was going to blow his head off."

She leaned forward. "You are making a poor choice."

"What choice? There is none. You came here to deliver an ultimatum. I don't respond well to those."

She stroked Oliver. "Perhaps this is not the time for this discussion."

"Now is not really all that convenient for me." I went into the kitchen and basted the bird with some more garlic and butter. "I would still like to see you." I chopped up the last potato. "It's supposed to be nice this weekend. Let's take Cynthia to the zoo." I carefully arranged the potatoes around the bird. "Let's eat and we can discuss this some more later. Chef James is in the house." I closed the oven and walked back into the living room. "I'm afraid I only have red wine…"

Robin was gone, and her key to my house was on my manuscript. I picked up the key and rubbed it between my fingers and thumb.

Susan stood up. "Ungrateful bitch."

"Maybe she's right."

"Maybe things are the way they should be now."

I looked at the Lion. "What do you think?"

He trotted around the living room, each paw raising, bending and plopping on the hardwood floor. Oliver watched him. The Lion stopped and sat down, his tail twitching. "Like I already told you--eat, sleep and get laid. Be creative. Embrace the hunt."

I set the key down next to Cynthia's gifts and gazed at the three place settings on the table.

Susan leaned over Oliver. "Oh for God's sake. I'm your punishment, stupid. Don't you get it?"

"Get away from him." I rushed toward her.

She laughed. "What are you going to do…kill me again?" Susan pointed at Oliver. He was panting. I went over and picked him up and sat down with him on my lap. His breathing was erratic, almost as if he had overdosed on speed. He sniffed at the aroma of the roasting chicken which had filled the room. The Lion nudged Susan's thigh with his nose. They slowly walked up the stairs.

I stroked Oliver until his body was cold. I don't know how long we sat there, but it was completely dark when I wrapped him in the ski jacket that he had claimed as his bed. I turned off the oven and then snuck out the back of my house with a shovel and took him to a little knoll that overlooked the lake, a place where he could watch the water fowl. I didn't really know what to say over his grave since my relationship with God had not been one of accord, but mostly one of mutual anger toward one another. I wished Oliver great stealth in stalking and hunting in his future adventures and asked him to come visit when he could. I placed a stone just above his grave and then sat down on the moist leaves and watched the fog drift over the lake. The houselights on the opposite bank appeared to be moving as they intermittently peaked through the cracks in the fog, and I felt as though I could walk out into the mist and disappear. A calming numbness filled me, a focused rage completely absent any guilt at all.

I walked back to the house, and despite the fact that Susan was civil enough to leave me alone for the moment, I went downstairs into my office and pulled up my novel on my computer and started to write a chapter about my major character killing a ghost.

Epilogue

Francis seen dat boy took my ax. Nice boy. Snucked up on Francis few times, knows he's only foolin'. His daddy give Francis food sometimes, axked if Francis need sompin'. He a nice man, always lef' Francis be. Francis worry when dey be startin' fires 'round the field with dem mules 'til he come to the fence and 'splain dat dey was killin' dem yeller jackets. Francis just calls 'em nasty flies. Francis needs to gets some bottles for the preacher, gets Francis some food. 'Spect dat boy took Francis' ax for the food his daddy give Francis. So Francis just lef' him be. Didn't really need no ax anyhow--just keep folks away from Francis. They stays away now even if Francis ain't got it. Francis can't chop wood no mo' no how.

When Francis gits back home, them squirrels be chewin' Francis stuff. I scaddled 'em out. Bunch of folk grabs Francis, bunch of white men, and throws Francis on the ground. They's read somethin' to Francis and clipped Francis arms like we done with them hogs.

Francis see's the Mrs. pointin' at Francis and dat boy with the long hair lookin' down at his feet. He didn't have dat ax no mo, but the man dat say he's sherf had it. It's all red. Dat's how it looked after Francis kilt squirrels with it. Figured dat's what dat boy done. Nice he give it back.

Didn't like where they's take Francis. Bunch of white men throws Francis 'gainst the bars, and Francis can'st do nothin'. Gots food though. Had to keep dem white boys away, squirrels eaten my stuff. Francis like's eatin' mo but miss the trees. Francis like's when dem acorns fall on the roof. Dem is squirrels is cute when they comes and gets 'em. Don't mind them mules no mo. They kinna nice. Folks be real mad, said bad things 'bout

Francis. 'Spect cause Francis kilt dem possums. Ate 'em though. Kill somethin', you eat it momma say. Momma be real sorry dat mule kick Francis. Francis doesn't know why, doesn't remember, but she say it done kick Francis in his head, and dat's why Francis doesn't know nothin'.

They takes Francis to some place one day, some big, white building. Had to take off Francis hat and all. Bunch of white folk talked, guess 'bout Francis. They takes Francis back, and them white boys in there lef' Francis be. Sherf come and takes Francis fishin sometimes. Says he likes Francis. He a good man. Catches them fish good. Francis doesn't feel so good at times. Sherf say ain't nothin' he can do for Francis. Folks was real quiet 'round Francis. Got some chicken steak and 'taters with gravy. They say it won't hurt none and dat the 'lectricty don't hurt. Them hot apples was the best dat Mrs. Mathis brung Francis. Sherf axked if Francis wanted sompin' fore Francis go. Said Francis can't wear no hat though. He nice. Give Francis a first cigarette. Didn't like it none.